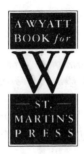

A WYATT BOOK for

W

ST.
MARTIN'S
PRESS

Books by Justin Scott

Mysteries

Many Happy Returns (MWA Edgar Nominee Best First Novel)
Treasure for Treasure
The Widow of Desire
HardScape

Thrillers

The Shipkiller
The Turning
Normandie Triangle
A Pride of Royals
Rampage
The Nine Dragons
The Empty Eye of the Sea (Published in England)

TREASURE
ISLAND

a novel by Justin Scott

A WYATT BOOK *for* ST. MARTIN'S PRESS
NEW YORK

Production Editor: David Stanford Burr

Design by Sara Stemen

LIBRARY OF CONGRESS CATALOGING-IN-PUBLICATION DATA

Scott, Justin.
    Treasure Island / Justin Scott.
        p.   cm.
    ISBN 0-312-11368-4
    1. Young men—New York (State)—Long Island—Fiction.   2. Treasure trove—Caribbean Area—Fiction.   I. Title.
PS3569.C644T73   1994
813'.54—dc20   94-32244
                                             CIP

First Edition: December 1994

10 9 8 7 6 5 4 3 2 1

For my nephew,
Justin Skelton:
Broadway bound,
via the West End.

PART ONE

FLINT'S MAP

1

The Old Sailor at the Admiral Benbow

SENATOR TRELAWNEY AND Dr. Livesey have asked me to write everything that happened on Treasure Island—but not to give away its actual coordinates, because we left a ton of loot behind. Start to finish, the senator demands. The whole bloodstained story.

So I go back to the 1950s, just before my father died. Back when doctors smoked and men were supposed to "watch their language" in front of kids; back when Mom said "the war" she meant World War II; back when we owned a run-down restaurant–tourist home on the Great South Bay called the Admiral Benbow Hotel.

One day we rented a room to an old sailor with a knife scar that split his face like a white-hot bolt of lightning. He was enormous. The Sayville Taxi's springs groaned as he climbed out and plodded up to our door—a tall, strong, sun-tanned man wearing a ragged old navy pea jacket and a naval officer's cap over his bristly crewcut. His hands were calloused and scarred, with dirty, broken fingernails, and I couldn't stop staring at the scar that mangled his cheek. But he was a sailor and reeked of boats and ships, and that was good enough for me, because I wanted to be a sailor too.

He cast a sharp eye at Fire Island, a low-lying North Atlantic barrier beach five miles across the water. Then he inspected the road past the ferries and the town dock that bordered our land, and the beach, which was strewn with seaweed and horseshoe crab shells and ribbed every few hundred yards by stone breakwaters. He whistled to himself as he absorbed the scene, then burst out singing a song that, in the months to come, turned out to have a zillion verses, each dirtier than the last:

> *"Oh, the monkeys have no tails*
> *in Zamboanga . . ."*

in a hoarse, tottering voice that sounded like he had led choir practice in every gin mill on the planet.

He banged on the door with the handle of a huge jack-knife he pulled dangling from a chain in his pocket, and when my father opened up, brushed past him and into the bar demanding a rum and Coke. Pop made the drink, and before he could stop him, the old sailor broke every liquor law in the state by carrying his glass outside; he inspected the beach again, and gazed out at the bay, sipping slowly the whole while, savoring it as if my father had poured VSOP Courvoisier from its special glass cabinet instead of house rum from the speed bar. He glanced up at our Admiral Ben-bow sign—a neon cocked hat, cannon, and anchor, left off in daylight to save electricity—and remarked, as if pleased, "Quiet joint."

"Busier in the summer," my father explained. "People come out from the city. Sometimes."

The sailor looked at him sharply. "But not in the winter."

Not in winter, my father conceded, looking failure, if not yet death, in the face: just the local bar crowd and a few dinners on Saturday night.

"Suits me fine, think I'll stay awhile—Hey, pal," he called to the taxi driver, "bring my seabag." The driver staggered under the weight of a huge duffel bag. The sailor heaved it onto his shoulder with one hand.

"I don't need much, just a square breakfast and a drink or

two. And I'm sure you won't mind if I stand watch on your widder's walk once in a while." He nodded at the railed platform high on the roof where captains' wives used to watch for their husbands' ships in this part of the country. "What's my name? You just call me Captain—Here." He reached into the pocket where he kept his jackknife and fanned six fifty-dollar bills in his hand like a magician. I gaped. That was three months' mortgage payments. "Report back when that runs out," he ordered, sounding as fierce and proud as old Admiral Benbow himself, whoever he had been.

Even though he was dressed like a bum, and had acted like a slob taking his drink outside without even asking, there was something in his attitude that said he was no ordinary sailor, but a real ship captain who expected men to jump at his orders. The taxi driver told us he had gotten off the train from New York and asked about quiet places to stay on the water. Assured that our Admiral Benbow was like a morgue, he chose to move in with us. Which was all we learned about our new guest.

He was pretty quiet, most of the time. He walked the beach every day with a powerful set of binoculars (which he told me, when he had had a few, that he had "liberated" from a German U-boat commander) or climbed the stairs to the widow's walk. At night he sat by the fire in the bar and drank rum and Coke, "easy on the Coke." When somebody spoke to him he would stare them down, and if the person persisted he would snort a kind of foghorn noise through his nose; people learned to stay out of his way.

Every day when he came back from the beach he would ask if any sailors had been by. At first we thought he was hoping to run into fellow seamen he could talk to, but it began to dawn on us that he was trying to avoid them. On the few occasions a sailor did stay a night at the Benbow (driving out from the Brooklyn Navy Yard with their wives, pretty women whom Mom told me never to talk to), the captain would give them a careful once-over from the door before he entered the bar; and even then he would stay quiet as a mouse the whole time they were there. For me, at least, there was no mystery about his wariness. I knew what was going on because he hired me to be his lookout.

Money, the captain had discovered, was the key to my heart. He had caught me at the town dock mooning over the love of my life—a sixteen-foot Cruisers Incorporated runabout with a lapstrake hull, a raked windshield, and a fire-eating twenty-five-horse Mercury outboard, the fastest motor you could buy in those days. The boat was for sale and he easily wormed out of me that I would do anything to swell my meager savings account in the Oystermen's Bank.

The captain cast a professional eye at the hard afternoon chop riling the bay beyond the creek, then steered my attention to another boat for sale. Although it was the same size as "mine" I had barely noticed it because it had an ordinary Evinrude engine and sissy center steering.

"It doesn't have a windshield."

"Look at her bow, Jim. Sweet as a knife. She'll cut the waves. That bathtub you're drooling over'll pound your guts out while this baby leaves you in her wake."

I didn't want to hear that and I guess it showed on my face. The captain glanced around. It was a cold fall day, with few boats left in the water, and the town docks deserted. "Hop in," he growled, stepping down into the boat he admired. "Show you what I mean." My mouth dropped open. Boarding someone else's boat without permission broke every rule I knew.

"I said hop in," he repeated in a cold voice that demanded instant obedience. Heart pounding, I climbed down from the dock. "Bail," he told me. "I gotta jimmy the lock."

I watched in total disbelief as he flicked a thin blade out of his jackknife and popped the padlock that held the bow chain.

"Bail," he growled again. I found the tin scoop under the seat and started bailing rainwater while the captain pumped up the fuel tank and fiddled with the outboard's choke and throttle. His big hands flowed over the machinery with contemptuous ease; one yank on the cord and the engine started with a growl and the heady smell of gas and oil.

"Cast off!"

I scrambled for the stern lines.

He backed out of the pilings and steered a brisk course down the middle of the creek, leaving more wake than was polite and nearly swamping the only other boat out, a low-sided duck punt. I cowered beside him as we passed the hotel, praying my parents wouldn't see me. As soon as we were between the stone jetties that sheltered the mouth of the creek from the bay, he opened her up. She leapt onto her plane, flat and smooth on the protected water. "Watch," he growled. Big waves were rolling past the mouth. We sliced through the first like butter, flaring thin sheets of water to either side. We cut a second to glittering spray.

"The reason she's got no windshield, kid, is she don't need one 'cause she's built right. What you want to remember is first check out the hull—the rest of that crap you can stick on any time—but you can't change the hull." He twirled her through a fast *S*. Gradually losing my fear of stealing the boat, I began hoping he would go all the way across to Fire Island and let me steer. But he turned on a dime and headed back for the creek. By the time we tied up, my dreams had shifted forever to the graceful little Lyman. "Costs less, too," he said, then made me an offer.

He promised me a five-dollar bill every Monday morning if I would "keep an eye peeled for a sailor with one leg," and tell him the moment I saw the man. Usually when Monday rolled around and I asked for my money he would snort and stare me down. But by the end of the week he would change his mind, "slip me a fin," "debrief" me on who'd come and gone, and repeat his orders to look out for "the sailor with one leg."

Five dollars a week to watch for a one-legged man seemed a pretty good deal, at first. I had slaved for less at a hundred odd jobs last summer, pushing a heavy mower over weedy lawns, painting, sweeping up shops. One blazing hot week I helped dig a cesspool in a yard too small for a bulldozer. That gut-buster left me ten bucks richer, with blistered palms and fingers, and sporting a couple of little muscles that looked like I had stuck acorns under my skin. So the captain's five dollars looked like easy money. Except that the one-legged sailor who worried the captain began to haunt my dreams.

On stormy nights, when the wind shook the house, surf thundered, and bolts of lightning painted tangles of whitecaps, I used to dream of crossing the bay in my boat to rescue sailors driven aground on Fire Island. Now I lay awake imagining what the one-legged man looked like: sometimes the leg would be cut off at the knee, sometimes at the hip; sometimes he was a weird monster born that way, with the one leg in the middle of his body. I'd see him leaping and running and chasing me along the beach, out on the slippery jetties, off the rocks into black water alive with horseshoe crabs and jellyfish. All in all my weekly five cost me a fortune in quaking nights and bleary mornings.

On the other hand, serving as his lookout made me less afraid of the captain himself, who tended to scare the daylights out of most people who came to the bar, especially when he had had a few too many rum and Cokes. He would start singing dirty sea songs at the top of his lungs—with verses I'd never learned in Scouts.

"Drinks around," he'd bellow, and make everybody sing along the choruses. Plenty of nights they'd rattle the Benbow's windows with "The monkeys have no tails in Zamboanga," with the captain bellowing fresh verses and

everyone singing along for dear life, afraid if they didn't he would notice.

He was pretty scary when he was drunk, quick to take offense and challenge anyone he thought disrespected him. He wasn't young, but he was a big man, and our neighbors, even the tough baymen accustomed to defending their clam beds with fists and rifles, knew a fighter when they saw one; the big scar on his cheek seemed to sneer, "I'm not afraid of getting hurt. I've *been* hurt. How about you, pal?"

Drunk, he was overbearing; nights like that he would pound the bar for silence if anyone interrupted one of his stories, then pound it louder when their attention wandered. And just try getting out the door before he was ready for bed.

His stories frightened people even more than his scar—terrible tales of submarine attack, men drifting in lifeboats, forced to drink their own urine and driven to cannibalism; salvage divers trapped in darkness, air hoses cut; shootings, stabbings, gunrunning, and torture. It was pretty clear that if half were true he had known some of the worst men in the world. His language was filthy, but nobody dared shut him up, even though the roughest clammer wouldn't talk that way in company.

My father kept saying he would ruin the hotel and frighten away our meager bar crowd, but in fact, horrible as the captain was, he sort of perked things up that winter. There wasn't much to do in town and not everybody owned televisions yet, so going down to the Benbow to get frightened was sort of a break in the routine. The drag racers and the leather-jacketed hoods who had dropped out of high school actually started looking up to him as the sort of "tough bastard" America had always needed to man her ships and win her wars, although even the captain had never claimed to be in the navy.

He began to ruin us, however, in another way. He

wouldn't pay his bill. The original fifty-dollar bills had run out, but he stayed anyway, keeping his room, demanding his bacon and eggs in the morning and his rum and Cokes at night. My father couldn't get him to pay. Now and then he would try, mentioning the money while he poured a drink, and the captain would give him a deathlike stare. If my father tried again the same night, the captain would pull his nose-snorting trick, roaring like a walrus until my father retreated, anxiously mopping the bar, and unable to meet my mother's eye. I really think that the stress of trying to cope with the captain and get the bill paid helped kill him.

The captain never changed his clothes, except once in a while he would send me into town to buy him some socks. His navy cap got a crack in the visor, but he never replaced it and it began to angle in front of his face like a gabled roof. He would sew his pea coat and trousers himself, and by the end they were less coat and pants than patches. He never got a letter and he never mailed one. Nor did anyone telephone him and he never spoke to a soul but me, except now and then in the bar when he was drunk. And no one, not even I, ever saw what he kept in his duffel bag.

He was only once crossed, and that was toward the end, when Pop's heart began to give him so much trouble that he went into the hospital for tests. We couldn't afford to keep him there long and he came home with orders to rest. Dr. Livesey made a house call one afternoon, then stayed for dinner with my mother, and after dinner went into the bar to smoke one of her French Gauloise cigarettes. I followed her in, and I remember noticing the contrast the neat, precise doctor, with her silken ash-blond hair and flashing dark eyes, made with our filthy, bleary-eyed bum of a pirate, slouched behind six empty rum and Coke glasses with his elbows on the table. Suddenly he started singing his song:

> *"Oh, the monkeys have no tails*
> *in Zamboanga . . ."*

By now none of us paid much attention to the song; it was new that night only to Dr. Livesey, who didn't seem to like it much. She looked up, quite annoyed at the loud interruption, then resumed her conversation with old Taylor, a retired gardener at the Trelawney place. In the meantime, the captain seemed to wake himself up with his own singing and began banging the table in a way we all knew meant silence. Everybody stopped talking, except Dr. Livesey; she went on, her melodious voice loud and clear, pausing between sentences for a puff of her pungent Gauloise. The captain glared at her for a while, banged the table again for attention, and not getting it, growled, "Pipe down belowdecks."

"You talking to me?"

Women doctors were rare in those days, particularly outside the cities, and she was a well-known and well-liked character on the South Shore. She had been a field nurse with Patton's army, lying about her age, and after the war had gotten her medical degree. Now and then some gossip would call her "hard" or "mannish," but she was actually rather delicately formed: I thought she was the most beautiful woman in the world, except for my mother.

The captain growled, "I don't see any other loudmouth broads in the joint."

"I have one thing to say to you," replied the doctor. "If you keep on drinking rum, Sayville will soon be short one fat slob."

The old captain was enraged. He sprang to his feet. Out came the jackknife. Flicking the blade open, cradling it open in the palm of his hand, he threatened to pin the doctor, "woman or no woman," to the wall.

Dr. Livesey barely moved. She started to reply as before, over her shoulder and in the same tone of voice, loud enough for the whole room to hear, perfectly calm and steady—but noticing me gawking from the kitchen door, she said first, "Jim, cover your ears." And when I did, leaving space under one hand to still hear, she said, "If you don't put that knife away, I'll have your ass in the Islip Town Jail in twenty minutes."

There followed a battle of looks between them, which the captain soon lost. He sat down, pocketed his knife, and grumbled.

"One more thing," continued the doctor. "I'll be watching for you. I'm a medical examiner as well as a doctor. Every cop and state trooper in Suffolk County knows I can do him a favor. If I hear one word about you causing trouble I'll make you wish you'd never heard of Long Island." With that, she stalked out, flinging her wool cape over her shoulders, fired up her Jeep, and roared into the night. The captain was quiet for the rest of the evening.

2

Black Dog Comes and Goes

SOON AFTER DR. LIVESEY faced him down, we lost the captain and inherited his enemies. The winter had turned bitter cold, with high winds and temperatures in the teens for days; the bay froze solid all the way across, then melted in storms of sleet and rain. My father—suffering a heart condition that's treated these days with routine bypass surgery but back then was beyond the doctors—got weaker and weaker, and soon my mother and I were running the hotel by ourselves, too busy to pay much attention to our nonpaying guest.

Very early one cold Saturday morning, when the beach was stacked with slab ice, the wind sharp, and the sun still so low it barely cleared Fire Island, the captain got up earlier than usual and headed out for his walk, his binoculars swinging from their leather strap around his neck and his jackknife glinting from his pocket. He had his cap pulled down over his eyes and his breath trailed like smoke. As he scrambled over the first breakwater, I heard him snorting with indignation as if remembering his set-to with Dr. Livesey.

My mother was upstairs taking care of my father and I was setting the table for the captain's breakfast when the front door opened and a man I had never seen before stepped in. On a morning anyone else would have been red with cold, his face looked pasty yellow. He took off his left glove, and I gaped. He was missing two fingers. A sheath knife was strapped above his ankle, but I had a feeling it was there for show or to make himself seem tougher than he was, because he certainly didn't look like a fighter. I'd been watching for sailors, to earn my five dollars a week, one-legged or two, and I remember being puzzled by this guy. He didn't look like a sailor, and yet he had some trace of the sea about him too.

I asked him what he would like, and he said coffee, but when I headed for the kitchen, he pulled his chair up to the breakfast table and motioned me over. I stopped where I was.

"Come here, kid. Come over here."

I took a step nearer.

"Is this here table for my pal Bill?" he asked with a kind of leer at the place I had set.

I said I didn't know his pal Bill, and this was for a guest in our hotel whom we called the captain.

"Well," said he, "my pal Bill would be called the captain, probably. He has a cut on one cheek . . . Helluva guy, especially when he's had a few . . . Let's just say, for argument's sake, that your captain has a cut on one cheek—and let's say it's the right cheek. Good, I thought so. Now, is my pal Bill in this here hotel?"

I told him he was out walking.

"Which way, kid? Where'd he go?"

I pointed toward the breakwater and told him when the captain would probably get back, and answered a few other questions. "Terrific," said the stranger. "Bill's gonna get a real charge out of seeing my mug."

The expression on his "mug," however, didn't suggest that the captain was going to be that thrilled at all. But it was none of my business, and besides I had no idea what I could do about it.

The stranger hung around the door, sneaking looks the

way our cat watched my mother's bird feeder. I stepped down to the beach for a look myself, but he called me back inside. And when I didn't obey as fast as he wanted, his yellowish face screwed up in anger and he ordered me inside with a curse that scared the hell out of me.

As soon as I was inside he started acting like before, half nice, half sneering, as if he knew some secret that made him better than anyone else. He patted my shoulder and told me I was a good kid and he thought I was really okay. "I have a boy your age," he said, "little guy just like you. Good kid. Important thing for boys is discipline—gotta learn to do what you're told. Now if you ever shipped out with Bill, you wouldn't have stood there to be told twice—not you. That's not how you sail with Bill. And there he is—son of a gun— my pal Bill, with binoculars around his neck, God bless 'im."

The stranger kind of backed me into the corner behind the front door, where it would hide us when the captain swung it open. I was scared, and even more frightened when I noticed that the stranger seemed scared too. He loosened his sheath knife, got the handle outside his pants cuff, and swallowed hard.

The captain walked in, banged the door shut behind him, without looking left or right, bellowed "Coffee!" and marched straight to the breakfast table.

"Hey, Bill!" the stranger called, straining to put a hard edge on his voice.

The captain spun on his heel. The color drained from his face. He looked like he had seen a ghost, or something worse, and I swear I felt sorry to see him suddenly look so old and sick.

"Come on, Bill. You know me. You remember your old shipmate, don't you?"

"Black Dog!" the captain gasped.

"Who else?" crowed the stranger, definitely enjoying himself now that he seemed to have the upper hand. "Black

Dog for sure, come to see his old pal Billy, at the Admiral Benbow Hotel. Good old Bill, we've seen it all, me and you, since I lost half a mitt." He held up his mutilated hand.

"All right," said the captain. "You found me. What do you want?"

"Right you are, Bill," returned Black Dog. "Hit the nail on the head. Why don't I have a shot of rum from this nice kid here, who I've come to admire like my own son. Then we'll sit down and talk straight, like old pals."

"The bar don't open till noon."

"Hey, you're staying here. They can serve you any time."

"Jim," the captain growled at me. "Pour him a shot. I'll take one too."

I wasn't supposed to. The liquor laws forbade kids in bars, but off on our own down by the bay in winter, my parents didn't worry too much about my occasionally helping out, if there weren't too many people around. I loved the stepped tiers of bottles with their silvery pour spouts, and I had known their positions by heart since I was eight.

When I got back with the rum, they were already sitting across from each other at the breakfast table—Black Dog with his chair arranged so he could keep one eye on his old pal and one, I thought, on the door, in case he had to run for it.

"Beat it," he ordered me. I left them alone and went into the kitchen and turned up the gas to heat the griddle for the captain's eggs and bacon, while trying hard to listen to what was going on out there. For a long time I could hear nothing but the low rumble of voices deep in the two men's chests. But after a while they got louder, and I began to pick up a word or two, mostly curses, from the captain.

"No, no, no, goddammit-to-hell no!" he shouted once. And then, "Electric chair? Then all fry, I say. Every damn one of you sons of bitches."

Suddenly they exploded in shouts and curses and the

next moment the table went over with a bang and the chairs after it, and then a moment's silence, both men breathing heavily, ended with a scream. I burst through the kitchen door in time to see Black Dog running full speed for the street, pursued by the captain. Both men had their knives out and red blood was gushing from Black Dog's left shoulder. Just as he went through the door, the captain raised his bloody knife high overhead and stabbed down to plunge the blade into Black Dog's back. It would have split his shoulder blades, if he hadn't hit the overhead sign by accident. The captain's knife smashed some neon letters and to this day, new people in town ask if "AL BENBOW" was an Arab.

That wild stab was the end of their fight. Black Dog hit the road and ran like the wind past the ferries, while the captain crouched in the doorway trying to catch his breath and staring up in amazement at the sign, which had stopped him from murder. He gave his bloody knife a bewildered look, then wiped it on his pant leg and closed it and shoved it back in his pocket. "Getting old," he mumbled, rubbing his eyes as if coming out of a bad dream, and shambled back inside.

"Jim," he whispered when he saw me gaping. "Rum." As he spoke, he reeled, and caught himself with one hand.

"Are you okay?" He looked like he'd been stabbed too.

"Rum," he repeated. "Jesus, I gotta get outta here. Rum! Rum!"

I ran to make him a drink, but I was so shook up that I dropped the glass and then the bottle and while I was rescuing it before the rum all spilled, I heard the captain fall. Rounding the bar, I found him sprawled full length on the floor. My mother had heard the fight and came running downstairs. We knelt beside him and raised his head. He was breathing hard; his eyes were closed and his face had turned white as snow.

We had no idea how to help him. I tried to pour a little

rum down his throat, but his teeth were as tightly shut as if he had lockjaw. Fortunately, just then Dr. Livesey came, to see how my father was doing.

My mother and I looked up from the captain's body. "He's been wounded. What do we do?" my mother asked, then added, "if I call the police, we'll probably lose our liquor license."

Dr. Livesey swept in the scene—the fallen captain and the scattered furniture—in one quick glance. Now she knelt and examined him more closely. "Wounded? No one's wounded. The damn fool's had a stroke, just like I warned him. Okay, Mrs. Hawkins, you run up and tell your husband I'll be there in a minute. I'll do what I can for this idiot. Jim, give me a hand."

She listened to his heart with her stethoscope, then rolled up his sleeve to take his blood pressure. While she wrapped his elbow I saw he had a huge forearm, bigger than Popeye's, corded with veins and muscle and tattooed all over. One of the tattoos was a faded heart with the word *Mother* draped around it. Another said *Billy Bones*. Another showed a hangman's noose, a big, thick rope with seven knots. Another, partly obscured by his sleeve, appeared to be a girl. When I tried to move the cloth to see more, Dr. Livesey covered it with her hand and said, "Jim, get on the telephone and tell the operator we need an ambulance."

"No ambulance," muttered the captain. Eyes popping, he tried to sit up, glaring about and growling, "Black Dog?"

"He ran away," I said.

The captain sank back. "No ambulance," he repeated, glaring at Dr. Livesey, whom he clearly remembered. "I'm okay. Can't afford a hospital and don't want one. Hospital'll kill me."

"Rum'll kill you first," Dr. Livesey said, "just like I told you, Billy Bones."

"That's not my name."

"I don't give a damn what your name is. Only I'm telling

you here and now, one glass of rum won't hurt you, but you can't drink only one. You're an alkie, Billy Bones. If you keep doing it, you'll die. I'm going to give you a shot to calm you down a little. And we'll get you into bed. After that, you're on your own. Just remember, as far as you're concerned, you spell rum D-E-A-D."

We got him upstairs and she gave him the shot and he passed into a sort of sleep. Then Dr. Livesey took me by the hand. "It's okay, Jim. He'll be just as good here as the hospital. Let him rest a week or so. No booze, at all. Another stroke'll finish him . . . Now let's see how your dad's doing."

3

Dog Tags

AROUND NOON I brought the captain some orange juice and some pills the doctor had phoned in to the drugstore. He was lying in bed where we'd left him, though he had propped himself up a little on the pillows. He seemed both weak and excited.

"Jim," he said, "you're the only one here worth a damn, and you know I've always treated you right. Slip you a fin every week like clockwork. But the thing is, pal, right now I'm sort of down and out. You're the only one I can count on. You'll bring me a little shot of rum, won't you, pal?"

"The doctor—" I began.

He cut me off, cursing the doctor in a weak voice. "Doctors are asses, every damn one of 'em—women doctors especially. What the hell does she know about seamen? I been in places hot as burning gasoline, my buddies dropping like flies with malaria, Japs bombing the shit out of the beach— what does she know about places like that?—and I *lived* on rum. It was meat and potatoes and mom and dad to me, and if I can't have a little shot of rum right now I might as well be dead, and when you smell my corpse stinking up your hotel, Jim, you'll know it's your fault and that damn lady doctor's." He kept at it awhile, cursing and yelling weakly. Then he started begging, and I didn't know what to do. "Look, Jim," he pleaded, "see how my hands are shaking. I can't stop 'em. I haven't had a drop today." (He had apparently forgotten the drink he had before stabbing Black Dog.) "That doctor's an idiot—probably just a nurse, pretending. I'd check her license if I were you. Yes I would. Listen, if I don't have a drop of rum—just a drop, Jim—I'll get the DTs. I seen some weird stuff already. I seen old Flint in the corner, just behind you. I seen the murdering bastard plain as day. If a big guy like me gets the DTs you look out, Jim, I'll tear the place apart. Look at the size of me. Look at this arm. Your lady doctor herself said one drink wouldn't hurt—Jim, I'll give you twenty bucks for a shot of rum."

He was getting more and more excited, and I was getting worried about my father who was really bad today and needed quiet. And Dr. Livesey *had* said he could have one, that one wouldn't hurt. But I didn't like the captain thinking he could bribe me.

"I don't want your money—except what you owe my father. I'll get you a drink, but only one."

Figuring his hands were shaking too much to hold a shot glass, I splashed some rum into an Old Fashioned glass and carried it up the stairs to him. He was watching, big-eyed, grabbed it from me and swallowed it down, sucking the last drops from the rim.

"Aye, aye, sir," said he, "that's better. Much better . . . Okay, pal, how long did the doctor say I was supposed to stay in bed?"

"At least a week."

"Son of a bitch!" he cried. "A week. I can't. They'll be here by then. Black Dog'll tell the bastards I'm here. Bastards who couldn't hang on to their own and now they want mine. I ask you, Jim, is that a way to act? I'm a very careful guy. I don't piss away good money. And I don't lose it neither; faked 'em out once, and I'll fake 'em out again. They don't scare me. I'll pour on the oil and pull the old double-cross."

As he was ranting, he had risen from the bed with great difficulty, holding on to my shoulder with a grip that almost made me yell, and moving his legs like they were made of lead. And all the brave talk about the "bastards who couldn't hang on to their own" was delivered in a voice so weak it was sad. He tried to catch his breath when he finally got himself seated on the edge of the bed.

"That doctor did me," he murmured. "My ears are ringing. Help me down, Jim."

Before I could, he had fallen back on his bed. He lay there awhile, silent.

"Jim," he said, finally, "you saw that seaman today?"

"Black Dog?"

"Yeah! Black Dog. He's trouble, but the ones who sent him after me are worse. A lot worse. Real hard cases. Now listen, Jim. I got a pal o' mine who's standing watch on my back, but if they get him and I can't get away, remember it's my seabag they're after. My duffel bag, in that closet. If that happens, then you get ahold of that damned lady doctor and you tell her to get her cop friends right away. Tell her to tell them if they get here fast enough they'll catch old Flint's crew—every damn one of them that's left."

I must have looked as confused as I felt, because he stopped raving a moment, fixed me with a stern glare, and explained what he meant as if I were some sort of idiot just arrived from Mars: "I was first mate. Old Flint's first mate. And I'm the only one who knows the place. He gave it to me in Savannah, when he was dying, just like I'm telling you right now, Jim. But don't squeal to the doctor unless you see that Black Dog again or a sailor with one leg—him above all. Keep your eye peeled, Jim, and I'll split with you half and half, I swear it on my mother's grave. Half and half."

He babbled on a while longer, his voice growing weaker and weaker, but right after I gave him the doctor's pills, which he swallowed without arguing, saying only, "If ever a seaman needed drugs, it's me," he passed out with a groan.

I figured I had to tell the doctor the whole story right away. I didn't know who the dead Flint was, but it sounded like he had hid something valuable and told the captain where. Considering how he had nearly cut Black Dog in half for trying to muscle in on his secret, I was afraid that if he woke up feeling better and decided he had told me too much, the captain would kill me.

But that evening, the ambulance came for my father, and he was dead by morning. Sick as he had been, it still seemed sudden and I forgot all about the captain. Too shocked and stunned to cry, much less understand the finality of our loss, I shambled through neighbors' visits, helping my mother arrange the funeral, and struggling, unsuccessfully I knew, to ease the pain that made her cry like a little girl.

The captain staggered down the stairs next morning, had a little to eat and a lot to drink, snorting and growling at anyone who asked him to go easy. At night, the mourning in our house was accompanied by hoarse choruses of "The monkeys have no tails in Zamboanga."

Still, he was weaker every day, so much so that we would have called Dr. Livesey if she hadn't gone to New York for a medical convention. He would wander outdoors into the cold now and then and stand staring at the bay, oblivious to the icy wind tearing at his tattered coat. Then he would stagger back along the walls of the buildings, hanging on to the shingles for dear life and moving as if each step would be his last.

Drunk most of the time, he sat with his big knife open on the table as if daring anyone to try and take it away from him. Or maybe he was afraid, for he would turn silent and stare off at nothing, much the way I and my mother did thinking about my father. I had a feeling he had forgotten everything he had told me or simply didn't care. It was almost as if his mind had passed beyond the things that had troubled him when he first came to the Admiral Benbow. Once he amazed us, breaking into a song not about the monkey tails, but a love song that my mother said had been very popular when she was a girl.

The day after the funeral an ice storm knocked out the power and the phones. The electricity came back on after lunch, but across eastern Long Island the telephones stayed dead, though none deader than ours, which the telephone company had turned off for nonpayment. The ice storm got us a snow day off from school, and that afternoon I found myself unexpectedly with time to stare out at the mist rolling in from the east. On the verge of tears for my father, I saw a strange man slowly approaching the inn.

Something was odd about him and I stepped out the door for a better look. He was big and hunched over, and tapping the road ahead with a white cane. Closer, I saw he wore dark green glasses. His head was hidden in the big hood of his duffel coat, which was big even on him, making him look like a huge, blind bear. For he was blind, hunched forward and tapping his stick like a bug's antenna, left and right and straight ahead in a three-stroke pattern to find space for his feet. He stopped in front of the inn and sniffed the wind and then called out in a funny singsong voice:

"Can somebody tell a blind man, who lost his eyesight fighting for his country—God bless Ike—where he is?"

"You're at the Admiral Benbow Hotel on the Great South Bay, Sayville, Long Island." (The big kids had put on a play called *Our Town* in the high school gym, and if he weren't so horrible looking, I might have added, New York, USA, Northern Hemisphere, et cetera.)

"A boy. I hear a boy. Well, thank you, son. Thank you kindly. Could you do me another favor and lead me inside?"

I was afraid to touch him, he was so awful looking, but he was helpless so I made myself reach for his elbow to help him through the door. The second I did, he grabbed my arm like a vise. I tried to pull back, but he was unbelievably strong and yanked me right into the rough folds of his coat. "Okay, kid. Take me to the captain."

"I can't."

"Oh yeah?" he sneered. "Maybe I can't break your arm?" He jerked hard on it and I yelled with pain.

"Please, mister. I can't for your sake. He's gotten real strange and carries a big knife. Another man came and—"

"*March!*"

I never heard a voice as cold and cruel and ugly. It was scarier than the pain, and I "marched," leading him straight into the house, into the bar where the captain sat slumped over his rum and Coke. The blind man held me tight in his iron fist, leaning so hard on me that I could barely walk. "If you don't want me to slit your throat and stick your leg through it, lead me to him. When we're in sight, tell him, 'Guess who's here, Bill.' "

He gave my arm another squeeze that nearly made me pass out. At that point, he was scaring me a lot more than the captain did so I opened the bar door and yelled what he told me to in a squeaky voice.

The captain looked up and a long day's rum and Coke seemed to slide out of him. I had expected him to be afraid, and I suppose he was, but he looked mostly ready to die. Staring stone sober, he tried to stand up, but he didn't seem to have the strength.

"Don't move, Bill," said the blind man. "Maybe I can't see, but I can hear the pulse in your throat. Okay? Now business is business, Bill. Hold out your left hand . . . Kid, take his left hand by the wrist and bring it near to my right."

The captain and I both did what he said. I could feel him trembling and I'm sure he felt me shaking too, as metal glittered in the morning sun. The blind man dangled a shiny disc on a chain and dropped it into the captain's palm.

"You got till ten o'clock," said the blind man, letting me

go and practically dancing through the front door as fast as if he had radar. I stood still, listening to his stick tap-tap-tapping away on the road.

It was quite a while before either I or the captain recovered. Then, just as I let go of his wrist, which I was still holding, he pulled his hand to him and stared into his palm. "My old pal's dog tags," he muttered sadly. I had seen my father's and I knew he meant military ID; everyone in the service wore them. "They got my last pal . . . He was watching my back, Jim. Now I'm all alone."

After a while he looked up at the clock. "Ten?" he cried. "Six hours. Don't worry, kid, we'll screw them yet," and jumped to his feet.

There, he reeled, put his hand to his throat, stood swaying a moment, and then, with a funny sound, crashed face first on the floor.

I ran to him, calling my mother. But there was no need to hurry. The stroke Dr. Livesey had predicted had knocked him dead. Then a weird thing happened; I had never really liked him and he often scared me, though lately I'd begun to pity him, but when my mother gently covered his face with a tablecloth I burst into tears. It was the second death I had known in a week. But I was finally crying for my father.

4

The Captain's Duffel Bag

R IGHT AWAY, OF course, I told my mother everything I knew. Mom was really mad and yelled I should
have said something sooner. But she didn't yell long, because we both knew we were in trouble. If the captain had
any money in his room, some of it was rightfully ours to pay
his hotel bill. But Black Dog and the blind man and the rest
of the captain's former shipmates were coming back soon,
and they would want to collect what he owed *them*.

The captain's orders to go get help from Dr. Livesey left
out one major detail: how was I supposed to leave my
mother alone in the house with a dead body in the bar and
the blind man hanging around waiting for Black Dog and
God knew who else?

For that matter, how could either of us stay? Every noise
in the house seemed like a tapping stick. The furnace rumbled on and we both jumped as if King Kong was snorting at
the door. We ran to the car without even stopping for our
coats, but Mom was so scared that she flooded the carbu-
retor and it wouldn't start. So, with the fog rolling thick in
from the bay shrouding the dim streetlights with dark halos,
we ran for help.

The road to Sayville was lined with summer cottages deserted for the winter. The wind rustled the cattails in the
marsh. And it howled among the dark ferry boats stranded

on their cradles beside the creek. Halfway to town, we saw a lonely yellow light in the window of old Mr. and Mrs. Crossley, who had converted their cottage to year-round use. We pounded on the doors. The Crossleys let us in, but after listening to our story, Mr. Crossley announced that anyone scary enough to frighten the captain to death was no one he wanted to meet.

The name Flint, which meant nothing to my mother and me, cinched it, particularly since the blind man had already frightened some children earlier in the day and sent a dog howling with a boot in its ribs.

"Call the cops," Mr. Crossley suggested, but the phones were still out. Finally, Mrs. Crossley sent her husband to drive to the police station in Islip. My mother explained we couldn't wait that long as the dead captain owed us a fortune in back rent and bar bills. "Wait for the police," pleaded Mrs. Crossley, and wait we should have. But my mother was afraid that the cops would impound the captain's belongings, along with his body, which meant months if not years of waiting to be paid what was owed and what we needed. We looked at each other and her mouth trembled. There were doctor bills and our telephone was already disconnected and Lilco would turn the lights off next unless we paid. And we were down to our last tank of bottled gas for the kitchen.

"We'll get it ourselves," she said at last. "Come on, Jim," and I ran after her into the night, proud of how brave she was.

We hurried back down the dark road. An eerie full moon came rising through the fog, red and scary and threatening to turn the dark that hid us bright as day. We held hands and ran silently, both, thank God, in sneakers, past the dark summer cottages, past the looming ferry hulls, past the rustling marsh. Then, suddenly, the Benbow's roofs chopped their familiar piece of moonlit sky, and seconds later we were safely inside.

"Lock the door," my mother whispered, and I did and ran and checked the back door as well, then rejoined her in the bar, where she was closing the venetian blinds. "Get a candle." I lit one, and we pulled off the tablecloth and had a long look by the flickering candlelight at the captain's body sprawled on its back, with open eyes glaring and one arm stretched out.

We knew he had padlocked the closet where he kept his duffel bag and always carried the key. My mother covered her mouth and gave a little moan. "I can't touch him," she whispered through her fingers. She looked beseechingly at me and I felt so grateful that at last I could do something to really help her—something like my father would have done—that I knelt instantly beside the enormous body and felt his pockets for the key. His friend's dog tag had fallen from his open hand. I picked it up.

"The key," cried my mother. "Find the key!"

"He said he had till ten o'clock." Just then the old humpback clock in the bar started bonging. We jumped at the sudden noise, but the news was good. It was only six. We had time before his "friends" came back.

"Get the key, Jim."

I went through all the pockets in his pea coat, and then his pants pockets, vest pockets, and even his shirt. He had some nickels and dimes, a shiny fifty-cent piece, the little sewing kit he used to patch his clothes, a pack of Lucky Strikes, a Zippo lighter, a pocket compass, and his big jackknife. That was it; no key.

"Maybe around his neck," said my mother. "Oh God, I hate this."

"I'll get it, Mom." Kind of holding my nose, I unbuttoned the top of his shirt and there it was, hanging from a lanyard, like the kind we braided in Scouts. I cut the lanyard

with his knife, and we ran upstairs with the key to the room
where he had lived so long, rent free. Mom fumbled the fat
padlock open and together we dragged his heavy duffel bag
out of the closet, hoisted it onto the bed, and turned on the
reading lamp to see what was inside. It had a stiff draw-
string, tightly knotted, though like the sailor's knots he had
taught me, it untied easily.

For a second we could smell a life at sea—salt, and paint,
diesel fuel, cigarettes and rum. It was packed meticulously,
so things came out the narrow throat as neatly as they had
gone in. And yet he had obviously used the bag for long-
term storage, the way we used our attic. First out was a
three-piece suit that had a double-breasted jacket and a
chalk stripe somewhere between a banker and Al Capone in
a gangster movie. Mom said it looked as if it had never been
worn. It was carefully wrapped in tissue paper, as was a
snowy white shirt under it, and a bright red necktie. A pair
of shiny black dress shoes were under them, in shoe bags.
We felt inside, but the toes contained only a clean pair of
silk socks, as luxurious as anything I had ever seen. Beneath
this never worn dress-up outfit was a wooden box with a
gleaming brass sextant inside. Other boxes held brass divid-
ers and a small chronometer that said "Made in England"
on the dial. Buried deeper was another set of even more
businesslike tools, a pair of automatic pistols with muzzles
wide as garden hose. There were spare clips for the guns,
which were perfectly oiled and polished, and their cleaning
kit.

Next we came to bits and pieces of stuff: strange bright
seashells, including a small pink perfectly formed conch; a
bunch of foreign coins; a stack of faded postcards spilling
from a rotted rubber band; and then a heavy metal bar that
looked like it might be silver, which wouldn't be much use
to my mother and me when it came to paying the phone
company. I've always wondered why a guy on the run,

which he had been most of his life, would keep the sea-shells.

Still looking for plain ordinary money we could take to settle his bill, we dug deeper into the now nearly empty bag. Down near the bottom, Mom pulled out a stiff old boat cloak that looked a little like Dr. Livesey's, although this one had seen better days and, unlike the unworn suit, had been faded by sun and salt until it looked like the old sail we kept for leaf raking in the fall.

"Hell's bells," said my mother, but I crawled into the duffel bag and there, all the way at the bottom, I found a flat bundle wrapped in a waterproof poncho, and a small leather briefcase, which turned out to be fat with money when Mother spilled it on the bed. She stared at the heap it made, then said sternly, for my benefit, I presume, "We'll take what he owes us, and not a dollar more."

That turned out to be a lot harder than it sounded, because when she dove into it, we discovered it was mostly foreign money. There were English pounds, German marks, French francs, and many strange currencies from South America. In fact, there were very few American dollars, which made it extremely hard for my mother to figure out what he owed us. I started getting nervous; it was taking too long. "Grab it all, Mom. Let's go," I pleaded, but she said, "We are not thieves. We'll take what's ours and only ours."

She was trying to remember how many francs to a dollar and I was listening hopefully for the Islip cops, when there came a tapping sound that levered my heart into my throat. I grabbed Mom's arm. It was the blind man coming back. "Oh, my God," my mother whispered. We listened to his tapping draw nearer and nearer, down the road, tapping the short walk from the curb to our front step, up the step, to the door itself. First he knocked. Then the knob rattled. Then the bolt shook in the frame. There was an angry bang of metal on metal, as he tried to force his way in, then silence. We listened hard, praying the door would hold, hoping he wouldn't go around the back and break the glass in the kitchen door. The stick started tapping again, tap, tap, tapping, and we held our breath, hoping he wasn't circling the house. At last, to our unbelievable joy, we heard his stick tapping his path up to the road. Slowly the sound died out.

"Mom, take it all. Let's go! He'll be suspicious about the locked door. He'll come back with his friends." Unlike me, my mother hadn't met the blind man face to face, nor felt his steel claw of hand on her arm. So maybe it was blissful ignorance that had her doggedly counting out the captain's foreign money, or maybe it was pure honesty, or maybe, finally, for one second, after a long, hard winter of being slapped around by fate, she was just glad to have an excuse to dig her heels in and do things her way. Whatever, she kept on stubbornly counting and figuring and recounting, while I prayed for the cops, and begged her to hurry. It wasn't even seven o'clock yet, she informed me, and besides, we were only taking what was ours. Just then we heard a sharp whistle from a ways down the beach. That was plenty for both of us. More than plenty.

"I'll take what we have," Mom said.

"And I'll take this," I said, and, figuring to even up any mistake she had made, picked up whatever was wrapped in the poncho, and ran after her down the stairs. A half-dozen flashlights were jumping jerkily along the beach as if a bunch of men were running full speed toward our hotel, and I saw the dim green running light of a big sea skiff beached on the sand. There was no way we could defend the hotel against six men. We ran out the door, started up the road, then veered into the darker safety of the boatyard where the ferries rested on their winter cradles. Behind us we heard the rumbling of powerful marine engines. The wind bore the staccato tap of the blind man's stick, and the moon pierced the last fading tendrils of fog.

"Run, Jim," my mother cried. Her eyes started rolling up in her head as if she were going to pass out. She shoved the money at me. "Run," she cried again. "I can't."

I remember wanting to yell at her for wasting so much time being so honest. Thanks to her we were about to be killed. But I couldn't yell at her, of course. Nor could I leave her. So I dove under the nearest ferry—the old *Flying Hornet* of rum-runner fame—and pulled her in after me as she half fainted. There wasn't much room. The cradle was low, and I could barely squeeze her under the barnacled hull. Being by far the skinnier, I got in a lot farther than Mom, and there we hid, only partly out of the moonlight and afraid to even whisper because we were well within earshot of the hotel.

5

The End of the Blind Man

I HAD TO know what the men were doing. So I slipped under the keel of the ferry and up the far side, with the hull shielding me from the hotel. I climbed the cradle onto the ferry's deck, from where, crouched behind her gunwales, I could see the road leading to the Admiral Benbow and the section of the beach where the sea skiff had landed. As soon as I was in position, six men came slogging up from the sand and hailed three who were running down the road. The three were holding hands; the moon lit the unmistakable bearlike bulk of the one in the middle: the blind man, running full speed and bellowing orders.

"Kick in the door!"

Three men charged the hotel. But instead of splintering wood, I heard startled shouts, for my mother and I had not stopped to lock the door behind us as we ran and what they found was a wide open door which minutes earlier the blind man had found locked. They paused a moment, but the blind man drove them on in a voice afire with eagerness and rage.

"In, in, in, you sons of bitches! What the hell are you waiting for?"

The rest of the gang obeyed at once, except for two who stayed with him. I heard nothing but pounding feet for a second, then a cry of surprise. *"Bill's dead!"*

"Search his goddamned body," the blind man cursed again. "Rest of you haul ass upstairs and get the bastard's seabag!"

I could hear their feet pounding the old staircase so hard our old house must have been shaking. In another second there were more astonished and angry shouts. The window in the captain's room banged open with a crack and tinkle of broken glass, and a man leaned head and shoulders into the moonlight and yelled down to the blind man below.

"Pew," he cried. "They got to him first. Went through his gear with a fine-tooth comb."

"Is it there?" roared Pew.

"The money's there."

"Screw the money, you lamebrain. Flint's chart, I mean. Is Flint's chart there!"

"We don't see it here nohow," yelled down the guy in the window.

"Hey, you in the bar. Is the chart on Bill's carcass?"

A guy stuck his head out the door. "Bill's stripped clean. Nothing's left."

The blind man danced with rage. "Wait a minute. It's—it's that boy. I should've gouged his eyes out. Find him! They were here a minute ago. The door was locked before. Spread out and find 'em. And bring me that little bastard."

"They were here, all right," called the one in the window. "They left a candle burning."

"Spread out and find them! Search the whole damned house," Pew yelled, banging his stick on the road. "Tear the place apart. They're in there someplace."

I could hear, and my mother must have too, from her meager hiding place under the ferry, the sound of our hotel being systematically destroyed by pounding boots, angry fists, and hurled furniture. Glass flew in ringing explosions, wood splintered, heavy objects thumped on the floors. Then, gradually, one by one, the men came out and reported we were not inside.

Just then we heard that same sharp whistle that had scared us earlier out of the captain's room. It came from up the road. Earlier it had been a signal to charge the hotel. But this time it was repeated twice more in quick succession and by the way the gang froze in place it was a warning that trouble was on the way.

"That's Dirk," cried the man who had been in the window. "Twice. Run for it!"

"Stay!" roared Pew. "Stay right there. Dirk's short on brains and shorter on balls. He wouldn't know trouble from a hole in the ground. Find the boy. If you want the chart, find the boy. He's got to be close by. Spread out and find him. Bastards. Search! Goddamn, if I only had eyes."

I looked down. I could see my mother's feet sticking out from under the ferry hull; she was wearing the white sneakers she used in the kitchen and they shone in the moonlight like rabbit ears about to be yanked from a hat.

Pew's angry shouts sent two of his men trotting into the ferry yard and pointing their lights in the shadows, but they kept looking toward the sound of the whistle as if they thought they'd have to run for it any second. The others just stood on the road, shuffling their feet and exchanging nervous glances while the blind man ranted.

"You've got your hands on millions," he screamed. "All you got to do is find the kid with the map. You'll be rich as kings, and you just stand there shaking? Christ on a crutch, there wasn't one of you had the balls to face old Bill, 'cept me, and I'm *blind*. And I'm gonna lose my shot thanks to a bunch of gutless wonders. I'm going to wind up crawling into bars and cadging drinks when I could be rolling around in a Caddy. If you had the guts of a goddamned Sunday school teacher, you could catch the little bastard."

"Hang on, Pew. We already got Bill's money," one of them grumbled.

"They probably hid the map already," said another.

"Why don't you stop bitching, Pew. Take the money and run."

"Run? Run, you scum?" Pew shrieked, and swung hard with his cane, which was a lot heavier than most blind men's sticks. He knocked the man nearest him right off his feet, swung wide and felled two more. The rest scattered, cursing back at him, threatening to break his legs, and fighting to grab ahold of his stick, which he wrenched back and swung again. This cursing, screaming battle saved my mother and me. The two shining flashlights around the ferry yard ran back to help Pew and soon the entire gang were too busy trying to kill each other to search for us. And then, suddenly, from up the road to Sayville came a low roar, muted at first, but growing swiftly louder until it drowned out the cries and shouts outside the Admiral Benbow.

Motorcycles. Immediately there was a gunshot from the same area as the warning whistle, which must have been the final danger signal, for the gang stopped fighting and ran in every direction, some into the marsh, some down the beach toward the sea skiff. All but Pew. Deserted, still raving, he pounded his stick on the road, groped with his hand, and screamed for his friends to help. Finally, he took a wrong turn and stumbled a few feet into the ferry yard, passing near me, and crying, "Johnny! Black Dog! Dirk? Don't leave me, boys. You wouldn't leave old Pew, would you?"

The motorcycles came down the road with blazing head-lights and howling sirens. It was a state police squad, five troopers. Pew realized he had stumbled wrong, whirled, and ran all the way across the road and fell into the ditch beside the marsh. Leaping from the icy water, he whirled again, onto the road, right in the path of the lead Harley Davidson.

The cop tried to save blind Pew, but there wasn't time and he hit him square, knocked him down, and ran over him with both wheels, which were as wide as car tires. Pew rolled halfway to his feet, then collapsed quietly, and lay still.

I jumped down from the ferry and ran to the cops, who had all stopped, stunned by the accident. Mr. Crossley came rolling up behind them in his old Mercury; he'd been driving for the Islip town police when he ran into the patrol, who'd been hunting drag racers taking advantage of the downed phone lines to lay rubber on Montauk Highway—drag racers my mother and I both silently blessed for inadvertently saving our lives that night.

The troopers were big, solid men—the second sons of North Shore potato farmers—but their broad faces showed horror at what had happened. The officer in charge, Sergeant Dance, fired up his bike and raced down to the beach, where the sea skiff had landed.

We could hear the boat grumbling into deeper water. *"Halt!"* Dance shouted. *"Police!"*

A voice called back—Black Dog, I think it was—warning him to stay out of the moonlight if he didn't want his head blown off.

"Halt," Dance ordered again, unsnapping his holster flap and starting to draw his gun. A rifle boomed with an orange flash and a bullet knocked the hat off Dance's head. The next instant the sea skiff's twin engines roared hard and her propellers bit and she was gone.

Sergeant Dance stood knee deep in the breakers, sadly watching its wake melt in the moonlight. "Lost 'em, dammit." The phones were still out, but he called one of his men over and told him to try to raise headquarters on his radio to get ahold of the Coast Guard. " 'Fraid they got away, Jim. Now, what's going on?"

As he worked the Harley up out of the sand, I told him everything that had happened, which made him feel a little better about Pew, who was, Dance noted when I was done, "not exactly an innocent victim."

Pew was dead as a doornail. Dance woke my mother up, breaking little capsules of ammonia smelling salts under her nose, then carried her back to the hotel, while she demanded to be put down, protesting she was fine.

The Admiral Benbow was wrecked. They had thrown every bottle off the bar and bashed in doors and smashed furniture, as if first searching, then mad they couldn't find what they had wanted. The place stank of spilled booze and the beer gushing from a broken tap, which I stopped by running down to the cellar to shut the keg. They had stolen the small change from the cash register, and the captain's money bag. Dance paused to look down on the captain's body. "What the hell were they looking for?"

I looked at my mother, who was shaking her head at the wreckage. There were bitter tears in her eyes, which told me as much as the broken glass and smashed tables that the hotel was ruined and we were finished. We had nothing but the captain's poncho-wrapped package, which I had stuffed inside my sweater.

Pew had kept yelling about a chart, a map. And I thought I had it. But I was afraid that if I handed it over to Sergeant Dance the cops would keep it. It was not easy for me to hold back; my mother and father were deeply honest people; they never cheated a customer, never padded a dinner check, never clipped a drunk out of his change. And they had taught me to believe that the police were our friends. Indeed, when cops did stop by Pop always poured them a free drink; Sergeant Dance had enjoyed the occasional beer to wet his whistle for the long ride back to Port Jefferson. But fresh in my mind was my mother's fear that the cops would have impounded the captain's seabag as evidence. So wouldn't they do the same with the package under my sweater?

On the other hand, hanging on to it alone could be very dangerous, if Black Dog and Dirk and the others came back.

So I said, "Dr. Livesey might know what they wanted. She spoke with the captain. He told me a couple of things when he died that she might understand."

"Dr. Livesey?" Dance perked up, took off his cap, and carefully combed his fingers through his hair. "Yeah. Let's go see Dr. Livesey. Come on, Jim, hop on the back. Mrs. Hawkins, I'll leave a couple men here. Give her a hand cleaning up, boys." With that, he stood tall on the Harley's starter, kicked the engine over, and motioned me onto the seat behind him. I didn't have to be invited twice. I wouldn't have cared that moment if they had burned the hotel to the ground, because a lights-and-sirens ride through the night on a Harley Davidson was about as close to heaven as I could imagine.

6

The Captain's Papers

I HELD TIGHT to Sergeant Dance's leather jacket as we roared off. Up to speed in seconds, the engine settled into a steady muted thunder. The heavy, well-sprung bike glided like a magic horse, the finely tuned motor vibrating under me as smooth as oil, the wind tearing past my face as if we three, me and Dance and the bike, were flying toward the moon. Behind us, blazing headlights, our troop held perfect formation, and I thought in that moment that when I grew up I would be a motorcycle cop instead of a sailor.

Soon, too soon, we were in Blue Point, pulling up in Dr. Livesey's driveway. Then, a reprieve. Her housekeeper answered the door; Dr. Livesey wasn't home. She was back in Bayport having dinner at Senator Trelawney's. And again we thundered into the night.

Former Senator Trelawney lived in a huge old mansion on the bay. His house loomed against the moonlit sky much bigger than our entire hotel. He had a long, curving clamshell driveway that turned through formal gardens and sweeping lawns. Bare, ghostly beech trees lined the drive and here and there I could see a statue gleam white, and the shiny surface of a fishpond, squared and rimmed with stone. There weren't many lights on. A butler answered the door after a long wait. He was wearing a sort of tuxedo. I had never seen a butler before, and Sergeant Dance apparently

hadn't either, because he took off his hat and started shuffling his feet as he explained he was on official police business to see Dr. Livesey.

The butler let us in and led us down a long, long hall and
into a gigantic two-story room with French windows over-
looking the moonlit bay. Between the windows was a huge
fireplace, with flames leaping from a mound of burning logs.
A shaggy bearskin rug was spread before the fire and to either side of it were wing chairs, into which were settling Dr.
Livesey and Senator Trelawney.

I had never seen the senator so close before, only once in
the bigwig's Caddy convertible in the Fourth of July parade.
He was a tall man, over six feet, and broad in proportion. He
had a big, open face, weathered from his travels and years in
the navy, so he might have passed for a bayman, except
there wasn't a slouch in him. His bold dark jumpy eyebrows
made you think he could move fast, and change his mind
even faster.

"Come in, Sergeant Dance," he said, beckoning casually
with one finger.

"Evening, Sergeant," said the doctor with a nod. "Who's
that, young Jim? Hello, Jim. What'd you do to fall in the
clutches of the state troopers?"

I knew she was kidding, but Sergeant Dance stiffened to
attention, assured her I had done nothing wrong, and reported what had happened as if explaining how the two of
us had been caught playing hookey from school. Senator
Trelawney leaned on the edge of his chair, listening in-
tently, and Dr. Livesey kept striking matches but forgetting
to light her Gauloise, as the story unfolded. She clapped her
hands when they heard how my mother went back to the
hotel for our money, and the senator said, "Smart woman.
That took guts." Pretty soon he was up and striding excitedly around the room, while Dr. Livesey gathered her long
blond hair in a ponytail and slipped a businesslike band
around it to hold it out of her face.

"Nice going," said the senator when Sergeant Dance had finished. "And as far as running over that blind SOB is concerned, sounds to me like he got what was coming to him. I'll speak to your captain in the morning."

Dr. Livesey said she'd better go have a look at the body, but Dance informed her that headquarters had already dispatched the chief medical examiner, so she sat back and reached for her brandy snifter, apparently forgetting that it was not on the table beside her chair, but on the hearth next to Senator Trelawney's, in front of the bearskin rug. Noting her confusion, he swooped across the room, scooped up both glasses and handed her hers. The red flush from the fire I had noticed earlier in her cheeks flared up again, bright as cherries. "Thank you, Senator," she murmured. "And done so discreetly."

"You did fine, Dance," the senator repeated. "And you too, kid. Hawkins, is it? Good kid. Push that bell, Hawkins, we'll get Sergeant Dance a beer."

I pushed a button in a wall covered in velvet and then Dr. Livesey beckoned me closer. "So you think you have what they wanted, Jim," she said quietly. "Can I see it?"

I pulled the poncho-wrapped package from my sweater and handed it over, glad it was out of my hands and safely into hers. She looked at it as if she were itching to tear it open, but instead just laid it quietly on the table beside her.

The butler returned with a glass of beer on a silver tray. Dance picked it up gingerly, then drained it in two nervous swallows, even as the senator was guiding him toward the door. "I'll take care of Jim," said Dr. Livesey. "Is his mother all right?" Assuring her that he had stationed two officers at the hotel for the night, Dance backed down the long hall and moments later we heard the Harleys fade down the drive. Soon the room was silent but for the crackling of the fire and the scratch of a match as Dr. Livesey finally lighted her Gauloise.

"Let's see it!" exclaimed the senator.

"Wait. Jim, did you have supper?"

I admitted I hadn't and she right away ordered the senator to have the remains of a pizza pie they'd shared earlier
heated up for me. The senator said his butler was heading to
bed and he would heat it himself. Telling him he would
only burn it, Dr. Livesey led me briskly down to the old
kitchens, popped the three slices into an oven big enough to
roast a pig, then carried them steaming back up to the fireplace room, where she sat me at a side table and told me to
dig in. I did. I was starving and pizza pie was a treat my
mother did not approve of.

"Now!" said the senator and the doctor simultaneously.

"Now," she laughed. "You know who Flint is, I'll bet?"

"Know him. Damned right I know. And you know I
know."

The two of them stood there, face to face, smiling broadly
and laughing as if they had finally heard the punchline to a
great joke. She turned to me, wolfing pizza as if I'd never
eaten in my life, and said, "Our war hero senator served
only one term in Washington, but before he retired—too
soon, say some—"

"But not you," the senator interrupted.

"No, not me. I like having you around. Before he came
home, he conducted hearings on the wartime black market
and contractor fraud. He knows the name Flint."

"Know him!" roared the senator. "Flint was a thief and
damned near a traitor. As far as I'm concerned you can
blame the *Normandie* fire on him."

Nuts for ships, I knew all about the French ocean liner
Normandie, the most beautiful ship in the world. She burned
and sank at her New York pier right after the Japanese
bombed Pearl Harbor. There'd been talk of Nazi spies at
the time—and years later a novel based on the same prem-
ise—but Senator Trelawney's committee had concluded
that naval idiocy and civilian corruption had doomed the
poor ship long before any German snuck aboard.

"And I blame him again for stealing the salvage crews blind when they tried to raise her. And that was during the war. After the killing stopped, then Flint turned to murder. Yes, I know him."

The senator dove into a huge stack of books and magazines teetering beside his leather chair. "Here!" He hauled out a several-years-old *National Geographic*, flashed the cover triumphantly, and thumbed it open to an article on sunken treasure. "Read this!"

"I will if you'll stop waving it like a flag," the doctor replied tartly.

"It's all in here," the senator crowed, still waving it so that Dr. Livesey's white brow began darkening like a thunderstorm. They had forgotten totally about me, by now.

She snatched it from his hand and scanned it rapidly. "Oh, yes. The famous disappearing Flint."

"Never found him or the treasure."

Flint had led a salvage crew, she read aloud, attempting to raise a Nazi submarine which had sunk fleeing to Argentina at the end of the war. (The war, as I've mentioned, meant World War II in those days, when America, England, and Russia banded together against Germany and Japan.) The submarine had been filled with gold bullion—"the treasure of Adolf Hitler," the *National Geographic* called it—thousands of ingots of melted-down gold, as well as a huge collection of confiscated jewels and silver. The National Geographic Society had underwritten the cost of modern diving equipment, but when their divers finally found the sub with their underwater cameras, the bullion was gone, as was their man Flint and twenty of his deep-sea divers. The rest of the crew were dead, drowned in the wreck.

"So the people who raided Jim's hotel were after money?"

"Money? Of course money. Are you deaf? What could they want but money? What do you think they'd risk their lousy necks for, but money?"

Dr. Livesey's eyes flashed. "I am not deaf, Sena*tor*, but it's a little hard to have a conversation with you when you get excited. Now if I could just get a word in edgewise, what I'd like to know is this: assuming for a moment that Jim's got a map here that shows where Flint hid what he stole, what kind of money are we talking about?"

"What kind of money? What kind of money? *This* kind of money: if Jim's package here is any clue to where Flint hid the gold, I'm going to New York to buy a ship, fit her out for salvage, and go get it."

"How much?"

"Five million in gold alone."

I hung on every word, hoping, praying they'd include me. I wanted to go to sea even more than to ride a motorcycle. Maybe if Dr. Livesey would take me, my mother might let me go. Except for school, I thought with a sinking heart.

"Let's open this thing up and have a look."

The poncho was sewn shut. Dr. Livesey got her bag from her Jeep, tossed her Gauloise into the fire and snipped quickly through the stitches. Inside were two things—a book and a sealed manila envelope, like the one my father's will had been in.

Dr. Livesey sat down and opened the book. The senator peered over her shoulder. I hovered behind him, stealing glances whenever the adults seemed too engrossed to remember it was time for a kid to be in bed. On the first page was just some scribbling like the stuff you doodle in your looseleaf: "Billy Bones" and "Mr. W. Bones, Mate," and a sketch of the same hangman's noose he had had tattooed on his arm, and then, what in hindsight looked like a desperate pledge, "No more rum," followed by "He bought it off Palm Key." I wondered who "he" was. "It" was probably a knife in the ribs.

"Nothing here," said the doctor.

"Turn the page," prompted the senator.

"I am."

The next bunch of pages looked like my mother's account book, except the figures listed were all income, with no expenses. And the figures were identified only by date and the occasional initial. Also, as the years went by—for the entries covered nearly twenty years—the sums got larger and larger. Early on was a flurry of amounts initialed *L*. Then a whole slew of different letters, then a bunch of *L*'s again. Then *SP*, and finally a string of *C*'s, ending five years ago. The captain had attempted to add it all up at the end, and had crossed out several totals until he got it right. This amount he labeled "Billy Bones' pile."

"What is this?" said Dr. Livesey.

"You'd know, if doctors didn't make so much money they didn't bother counting it," said the senator. "It's the SOB's account book. The money he stole over the years. See all these *L*'s? That's *Lafayette*. That's what the navy renamed the *Normandie* while we tried to refit her as a troop ship. See, here's the date she burned, February 9, 1942. Then here the *L*'s pick up again when he came back to steal from the salvage job."

"What's *SP*?"

"Well, most American salvage men today learned their trade raising the *Normandie*. The navy set up diving schools on board the wreck. Then after they raised her, the salvors were sent on to clear the harbors we won back from the Nazis and the Japs." (My father had taught me not to, say "Japs." But he had been the exception, as most World War II veterans still called the Japanese, Japs.)

"*SP* could be South Pacific," Senator Trelawney continued. "Then *C* would be Caribbean, after the war, diving for the U-boat. The dates seem to fit. . . . At any rate, it's a record of every dime the bastard stole. Too bad he's dead. We could throw him in jail for the rest of his life—What else you got there, Doc?"

She had found a conversion table my mother could have used earlier for exchanging French and English and American money. "Clever bastard," growled the senator. "Wasn't about to get cheated by foreigners. What's in the envelope?"

Light flashed from Dr. Livesey's scalpel. She slit the flap and out fell a map of an island with latitude and longitude and channel depths and names of prominent hills and bays and inlets and all the bearings necessary to bring a ship safely into anchor.

The island was about nine miles long and five wide— shaped sort of like a fat dragon standing on his hind legs. It had two protected harbors, each almost totally landlocked, and a high hill in the middle, marked *Telescope Hill.* There were three red crosses, two in the north part of the island, one in the southwest. Beside the southwest cross, someone had written in the same red ink in a small, neat hand, totally different from the captain's tottery-looking notes: "The German gold is here."

Dr. Livesey exchanged a long look with Senator Trelawney, then turned the map over. On the back the same person had written some additional information:

Tall tree, Spyglass shoulder, bearing a
point to the N of NNE.
Skeleton Island ESE and by E.
Ten feet.
The jewels and silver from the Med
job is in the North hole; you can
find it on the slope of the east
hummock, ten fathoms south of the
black rock with the face on it.
The guns and ammo are easy to
find in the sand hill, N point of
north inlet cap, bearing E and a
quarter N.
                                            J F.

That was it; but brief, and baffling as it was to me, it thrilled the senator and Dr. Livesey, who said, "J.F. John Flint."

"Doc," said the senator, "give up your measly practice. Tomorrow I'm heading in to New York to buy the best ship and crew in the States. We'll take my driver Redruth, and Joyce, and Hunter. We'll make the Caribbean in a couple of weeks and before you know it we'll all be rich as kings."

At last he noticed me skulking like a second-string right fielder praying to get into the game. "You want to come along, Jim?"

"Oh," I said.

"You want to go treasure hunting, Jim?" he prompted. "You can be our cabin boy. You'll be a great cabin boy. Get my friend Doc here to deal with your mom."

"Senator," said Dr. Livesey, "I'll go with you. And I'll talk to Mrs. Hawkins—tell her it's good for the boy to get away. But there's one man I'm afraid of."

"Who?" demanded the senator with a protective glare that left no doubt where the doctor lay in his heart. "Name the bastard. I'll tear his head off."

"You."

"Me?"

"You've got the biggest mouth on the Great South Bay. We're not the only ones who know about this map. So does the gang that wrecked the Admiral Benbow. We'll have to protect Jim and his mother. But the main thing is, keep your trap shut."

The senator puffed up and his face got purple.

"Don't tell anybody what we've found. Promise?"

At last he nodded ruefully, patted her shoulder, and said, "You're right, as usual, Doc. I'll be silent as a tomb. Not a word will pass my lips. Don't worry. I won't tell a soul. Wild horses couldn't drag it out of me."

PART TWO

THE COOK

7

I Go to New York

FINDING, OUTFITTING, AND crewing a ship took longer than Senator Trelawney had promised. Dr. Livesey, who had quickly arranged for a replacement to cover her practice, and another to fill in and take over her assistant medical examiner duties, got impatient. She had even rented out her house and was forced to move into one of our rooms, which made my mother happy to have the company and the rent.

For me, every delay was a godsent piece of luck, for while my mother had allowed herself to be convinced that I would do fine in Dr. Livesey's care, nothing could have persuaded her to let me out early from school. The spring crept by, and each week I lived in fear that word would come that Senator Trelawney was ready to sail without me.

He had pulled a couple of the strings he was famous for, and many of my mother's troubles had evaporated. The bank that held the mortgage on the Admiral Benbow turned positively friendly after a call from the senator, and a crew-cut vice president had actually visited to explain that they were in no rush and were more than willing to wait until my father's life insurance came through. At the same time, a couple of men who worked on the Trelawney place stopped by in the afternoons to repair the damage Pew's gang had done to our doors and windows. Old Taylor's gardeners came over in a truck and when they had gone we had azaleas blooming around the front door and a rugged row of cypress trees protecting the parking lot with a welcome windbreak.

Best of all, one of the charity foundations Trelawney directed sent a pair of very pleasant recovering alcoholics to live at the hotel and they turned out to know the hotel business and be a big help to my mother, Doris taking over the kitchen, Joe tending bar with a flair that charmed back our regular crowd. Redruth, the retired cop who drove the senator's car, moved in too, just in case Pew's gang took another crack at us. He was large and grouchy, with permanently beetled brows and eyes that tore right through you.

By late May it looked as if I would actually be able to join the treasure hunt. And, as it worked out, I was just finishing final exams when Dr. Livesey got a letter from the senator.

In my excitement, I missed at first the twin dots of red color in her cheeks and the fact that she was literally grinding her teeth. "Read that," she growled; then, greeting my mother warmly, said, "Jim'll be back in time for school if I have to send him parcel post."

I yanked the letter out of the envelope and read eagerly. "Janet," it began,

> Hope you've got everything sewed up, because we are ready to go. Grab Jim and hop a train to New York. The ship's a beaut, even though she's named *Hispaniola*—I would have preferred something a little more American sounding, but I suppose it'll be fine in the Caribbean. She's a full-fledged salvage tug, seagoing, a hundred and twenty feet with a diesel engine big enough to drive a locomotive. I lucked into her. Blandly, a guy I knew in the Pacific, found her. She's got a towing winch, compressors, and plenty of diving gear, none of which we'll probably need, but the price was right. There's a one-inch gun on her

bow, since she was outfitted as a sub chaser, and cabins for us and a fair-sized fo'c'sle for the crew, decent galley, and a new generator. Best of all, she's got modern controls so one man can run her from the bridge, which eliminates a lot of engine-room crew. Like I said, she's a beaut, so when certain people tell me that Blandly bought her for a song, navy surplus, and pretended to find her just for me, I laugh. He was also helpful getting crew, including a heck of a captain—Smollett—tough SOB from the old school. Crew, however, was a bit of a problem, until the word got around what we were sailing for.

I looked at Dr. Livesey. "What word got around?"

"The senator was apparently trampled by a wild horse," came her thin-lipped reply. I read on:

After that, they mobbed the place. I was interviewing twenty men a day and felt myself getting in over my head. Fortunately, a guy came to my rescue. He used to be a captain himself till he lost his leg at Iowa Jima and he retired and opened up a tugmen's saloon over on Staten Island. I ran into him at the dock where we're fitting out the *Hispaniola*. The poor guy came limping along and we started talking and he admitted right off he misses the sea so much that he occasionally comes down to the dock on his crutches just to smell the salt. I knew what he meant; I'd have gone nuts these last years if I couldn't step out of the house to smell the bay—even though it's just a glorified mud puddle. Anyhow, we understood each other right off. His name's Long John Silver.

The "Long," I imagine, stands for "long on guts," because he was driving an ammunition ship at Iwo. When I asked around about him I heard that his bar does a pretty good business, but the navy apparently screwed up his pension and lost all his records—so it's not exactly a carefree retirement. Can you imagine that? Lost a leg at Iwo Jima and he's left to fend for himself. Goddamn government. Glad I'm out of it. I also got the impression that Long John could stand some vacation time from his wife, who runs the bar with him, which a couple of old bachelors like you and me can understand, eh Janet? Ha ha.

"Ha ha," Dr. Livesey repeated under her breath.
"Anyway," the senator's letter continued,

Long John Silver offered out of the blue to sign on as our cook. I nearly fell over, but he was serious, and not only that, he saw right away the trouble I had sorting out the crew.

He knows the New York waterfront like the back of his hand and he knows New York seamen. So he went through job applicants and rounded up a hell of a bunch, including a first mate named Arrow. Then he looked over the men I had hired and recommended firing a couple of them, pointing out that they were just tugboat deckhands looking for a quick buck. And before I could worry about it, he had replaced them with his own boys. They're a little rough-looking, you'll probably notice, but they know their business—blue-water sailors every one—so the ship's in good hands.

Silver tried to persuade me to get rid of Captain Smollett and take command myself, but I told him that with the treasure to worry about as well as the ship, I'd do better as "admiral" of the entire operation, and Silver agreed immediately that I was right. So we're ready.

Tell Redruth to leave the car and join you on the train. And get here as soon as you can disentangle young Jim from Mrs. Hawkins's apron strings. He got us the map, after all—he deserves to join in the fun. Tell Mrs. Hawkins for me that it'll do the boy a world of good to get away for the summer. Remind her that *I* shipped out the first time when I was about Jim's age—scandalizing my parents, of course—and I've never regretted it. There is nothing like going to sea to turn a boy into a man, not to mention teaching him how to read his fellow man's character at a glance.

Yours,
John Trelawney

Early next morning, Mom drove us to the railroad station. She and I had already said goodbye at breakfast; she told me to obey Dr. Livesey and have a good time. I think she had convinced herself—with some help from Dr. Livesey—that our hunt for Flint's gold would be a sort of Boy Scout camp afloat. She hugged me again at the train—fiercely for a rib-crushing moment—then stepped back, brushing at her eyes. Up until then I was so excited to be going, that I felt no other emotion. But seeing her standing there, looking suddenly small and alone, I started blinking too.

"Buck up," Redruth grumbled. "Be a man."

"Ass," Dr. Livesey hissed at him. She threw an arm around my shoulders, but I had already mastered the tears. I waved once from the window and then the whistle blew and the train was picking up speed.

Half an hour later we changed to the electric train at Babylon. Redruth smoked and stared out the window, scowling suspiciously the closer we got to the city; Dr. Livesey read the *Saturday Evening Post.* I read the Classic Comic "Kidnapped," then watched, fascinated, as the train rumbled through longer and longer tunnels. Finally, we descended under the East River and ten minutes later got off in Pennsylvania Station. They had electric eye doors there that automatically opened when we approached. We followed signs to the subway, rode it to the Battery, roaring and banging underground, then emerged at Bowling Green and walked to the Staten Island ferry.

Skyscrapers crowded behind us, but ahead, a vast harbor spread east and south, broad and flat and peppered with ships and boats of every size. The Statue of Liberty, tall and green, watched over all this, all but ignored by the ferries, freighters, hooting tugboats, gray warships, and sleek liners. As soon as we boarded, I ran to the front of the ferry. It seemed big enough to carry thousands. There, by the gates at the bow, I stared. To a kid from Long Island, the sheer numbers of people and ships and the buildings towering over Manhattan Island behind us were almost overwhelming.

The Port of New York in those days looked like one of those picture books called *The March of Transportation.* On the Jersey side gigantic train yards marked the terminus of every important railroad in America. At the water's edge, trains were rolled onto barges, which tugboats hustled across to Manhattan and Brooklyn. Other barges—hundreds, thousands of them—took cargo from ships riding anchor, and tugs shuttled them from pier to pier.

Redruth came up behind me, and shoved a Peter Paul Mounds in my hand. "Dr. Livesey says eat this and don't fall overboard."

I saw ships from Europe, and Asia, and Africa. We passed one wafting the fragrance of coffee beans, another of sugar. A U.S. Navy aircraft carrier steamed by, its decks bristling with Corsair fighters. Then a great liner came downriver from the midtown superpiers. As it passed lower Manhattan, it thundered a signal on its whistle that shook the sky. I recognized the ship instantly by its two thick stacks—the brand-new *United States*, bound for England at thirty-five knots. The last time I had been to New York—the only time, other than our United Nations visit—my class had toured the *United States*. I knew she had been designed by William Gibbs, the man who created the beautiful *America* before her, and I remember feeling proud that she and not one of the fancy British *Queen*s was the fastest liner in the world.

People always talked about the Manhattan skyline—such a cluster of tall buildings was special then, even unique— but for anyone who loved ships and the sea, New York was the ultimate harbor. There was smoke everywhere, twirling white and billowing black from ship stacks, ferries, tugs, and lighters; booms swayed like forests above the freighters; and sailors from twenty nations scrambled on their decks.

Senator Trelawney was waiting at the ferry dock. He welcomed me and Redruth, grinning his biggest grin for Dr. Livesey. He was wearing a kind of blue officer's uniform and had a white peaked cap, which he tipped to the doctor with a private wink. "You look like you've re-upped," she said, smiling back. "Have you enlisted, Senator?"

"No, Doc. We're sailing on our own. No navy, no government, no rules. Just us and the sea. Did you bring the map?"

"Of course I brought the map."

"Hidden?"

"Very."

The senator's eyes flickered toward a bulge under Dr. Livesey's summer blouse. "A treasure hunt," he smiled.

I couldn't stand to wait around anymore, and even stolid Redruth was impatiently shifting his big feet. "Is the ship all ready?" I asked. "When do we sail?"

"Sail?" Trelawney bellowed. "We sail tomorrow."

8

The Binocular Bar

ALL THROUGH BREAKFAST the next morning, the senator kept getting up to telephone Long John Silver, but the line was always busy. Finally he scribbled a note inside a book of matches. "Jim, run this over to the Binocular Bar. It's just down the terrace."

"No," protested Dr. Livesey. "Not alone."

"It's not like the boy's never seen the inside of a gin mill," Trelawney retorted. "He'll be fine. All these tough-looking characters are just working guys. Go on, Jim."

I charged out the door without even finishing my eggs. I couldn't believe my luck, but here I was running down tugboat row—Richmond Terrace—beside the Kill Van Kull. The kill was a broad canal, thick with ships and tugs, and rimmed with docks, piers, barges, shipyards, and warehouses. There were sailors everywhere, hook-wielding longshoremen, deckhands and greasy engineers. Tattooed arms bounded, and I even saw a man with an earring.

The Binocular Bar was doing a roaring business for nine in the morning, busier than the Admiral Benbow on our best Saturday night. Sailors and longshoremen stood two deep at the bar and crowded the tables. They were all bigger than Sayville's biggest clammer, and yelling at the top of their lungs. A little afraid, and made homesick by a whiff of spilled beer, I hung by the door while my eyes adjusted to the dim light and the smoky haze.

A big blond man was wandering around like he owned the place, stopping to talk at tables, slapping customers on the back, gesturing for the bartender to pour rounds on the house, but he couldn't be John Silver. He had two legs, though he did carry a thick cane. Suddenly he roared laughter at someone's remark and emphasized the joke by banging the cane against his right leg. A hollow boom started the laughter again.

It was him, Long John Silver, clumping around on an amazingly real artificial leg. Only when I looked closely could I see how the cloth of his pants leg lay flat on the bend of his "knee."

Now, obviously, when Senator Trelawney had written about John Silver, my first thought had been of the one-legged sailor that the captain had paid me to look out for. But one look at this open-faced, cheerful guy was enough to make me stop worrying. He was big, with immense shoulders and a huge head, but he looked, compared to Pew and the gang that had wrecked my mother's hotel, as kind and honest as a Methodist minister. I weaved my way through the drinkers, and went right up to him with Senator Trelawney's note.

"Mr. Silver, sir?"

"What's up, kid—say, how'd you get in here?" He took the matchbook, read the note. "Oh, yeah. The senator's cabin boy. Heard about you—good news travels fast, huh? Hey, you want a Coke? Charley, pour the kid a Coke." And he shook my hand in his big strong fist.

A customer draped over the pay phone in the back turned around, saw me, hung up hastily, and hurried out the door. I couldn't believe my eyes. "It's Black Dog!" I yelled. "Stop him!"

"Hey," Silver yelled. "He didn't pay his tab. Harry, catch that son of a bitch."

A guy near the door jumped up and ran after him.

"It's Black Dog," I yelled again.

"I don't care if he's Admiral Halsey, he's still going to pay his tab. I'm not running a charity here." Silver finally let go of my hand and asked, "Who'd you say he was? Black something?"

"Dog," I said. "Didn't the senator tell you about the gang? He was one of the ones who wrecked my mother's hotel."

"In my bar? Jesus H.—Ben, go help Harry." He looked around with a dangerous glint in his eye. "Hey, Morgan. Were you drinking with that son of a bitch on the phone? Come over here."

The guy he had called Morgan, an old sun-browned sailor with a stub of cigarette smoldering from his lip, shuffled up, looking like he wished he was elsewhere.

"Now Morgan," said Silver, very firmly, "you never saw that son of a bitch before, did you?"

"Nope."

"You didn't know his name was Black Dog, did you?"

"Nope."

"Lucky for you, is all I can say, Morgan. 'Cause if you did, I'd bar you from my joint for the rest of your life. What was he saying to you?"

"I don't remember."

"Don't remember? Maybe you don't remember you know him? Come on, spill it. What were you talking about?"

Morgan shifted his weight. "We was talking about the gas chamber versus the electric chair."

"From personal experience, I presume?"

"Nope. We only been to hangings."

"Christ on a crutch. Go back to your table—Charley, get Morgan a beer, huh?"

And then as Morgan shuffled back to his table, Long John Silver made me feel a lot better by confiding in a quiet whisper, "Tom Morgan's a straight enough guy, but he was behind the door when they was handing out the brains. Now, let's see. Black Dog. Black Dog? . . . No, I don't know the name, but funny thing is, I think I've seen the guy before. You know, I think he's the same guy used to come in with this blind beggar."

"That's right," I agreed excitedly. "The blind man's name was Pew."

"Yeah! Pew. Hasn't been around in a year, if it's the one I'm thinking."

"He was killed by a motorcycle."

"That's the best news I've heard in a week. He was one sneaky bastard—excuse my French, kid. I'm not used to having a little guy around. Though you're not that little—plenty tall for a cabin boy, a real hotshot. You'll come home chief mate if you're as smart as you look, hotshot. Well, won't the senator be happy when we catch Black Dog? Ben and Harry will make mincemeat out of him. Talking of hanging, was he? I'll hang him."

He kept banging his cane against his hollow leg as if excited by the prospect of personally delivering Black Dog to the senator. I watched him closely, however, because it struck me that John Silver having only one leg and Black Dog just happening to be in his bar was a bit too much of a coincidence. Just then Ben and Harry ran in all out of breath. "Got away," they gasped. "Jumped a tug. He's in Brooklyn by now."

Silver was suddenly a very frightening sight—dark in the face and red in his eye. Ben and Harry backed away, exchanging worried glances, and I felt the entire room brace for an explosion. His voice was cold. "Here I have this confounded son of a Dutchman sitting in my bar swilling my booze and *you* let him get away? Beat it!"

Harry and Ben fled. John Silver turned to me, confiding, as he had earlier, "What in blazes is Senator Trelawney going to think? You spot the bastard and my boys let him get away. He's going to think the worst, is what he's going to think, and he's going to fire me before we even sail." His anxious eye fell on me and he brightened a little. "Jim. Could you put in a word for me? Look, kid, if I had two legs, I'd have nailed Black Dog halfway to the door."

Sad and angry, he banged his stick on the artificial limb. "Before I lost this leg, there wasn't a sailor in any navy could have pulled that stunt on me. I'da been on him like a shark . . . But that's not how it is with me anymore—"

Suddenly his jaw dropped. "Son of a bitch! Three shots of booze. The bastard stiffed me!"

And he started laughing so hard he had to lean on my shoulder. Then he sank to the nearest chair, bellowing laughter until the tears ran down his cheeks. I started laughing too—it was impossible not to—and soon the whole bar joined in, with men banging tables and pounding their thighs until Ben and Harry peeked back through the door they had just exited.

"Shark?" he cried at last, wiping his cheeks. "Shark? More like a trained seal with a gimp flipper is what I am." He shoved the big handkerchief he'd used to dry his tears back into his pocket and looked at me. "We'll get on great, kid. A trained seal and a hotshot cabin boy to keep him out of trouble . . ." His laughter died. "Speaking of trouble, duty is duty and I've got to haul my carcass over to the senator and come clean. Gotta tell him I blew it and face the music. Take my medicine like a man. No joke, Jim. Serious stuff—and neither of us comes out of it exactly shining, do we? . . . Nothing to do but make a clean breast of it and hope the senator understands."

My face fell. If he was in trouble, so was I.

"Hey, buck up, hotshot. Maybe it's too late for him to hire a new cook and cabin boy. Besides, he seems to me like a fair man . . . Jeez, I got stiffed by a louse I never should have served in the first place. But that's the bar business, ain't it?" And then he started laughing again and I joined in;

I didn't really get the joke, but I would have felt a little dumb just standing there with questions on my face.

We had a great walk back to Senator Trelawney's hotel. Silver knew everyone we passed and knew their ships. He pointed out everything that was going on, the cargoes that the ships were loading, the dry-dock repairs, where they were sailing, and told me stories about the ports they hailed from. When I'd look blank at some nautical phrase, he would repeat it, explain it, and wait until he was sure I understood before he went on. I knew he would be a wonderful teacher to sail with, provided Senator Trelawney didn't fire him and send me home to my mother for letting Black Dog get away. "Buck up," Silver repeated when we reached the hotel. "We'll ask the mercy of a good man."

Senator Trelawney and Dr. Livesey were waiting impatiently in the little lobby, the doctor smoking a Gauloise, the senator riffling through some invoices from Blandly's shipyard, which had done the refit on the *Hispaniola*.

Long John told them exactly what had happened, checking with me on every pertinent detail, asking, "That's what happened, right, Jim?" He left nothing out and I confirmed every word.

The senator and Dr. Livesey were clearly disappointed that Black Dog had got away, but to my relief neither suggested that Long John and I were at fault. Having made a "clean breast of it," Long John left.

"All hands aboard by four this afternoon," the senator called after him.

Long John pivoted on his walking stick and snapped a navy salute. "Aye, aye, sir. I'll be there with bells on."

"Well," said Dr. Livesey. "What do you think?"

"What do *you* think?" the senator asked back, with an anxious glance at the doctor.

"Generally speaking, I don't put a whole heck of a lot of

faith in your discoveries, but this Long John is fine in my book."

"I knew you'd like him," Senator Trelawney crowed happily. "The man's a prince . . . Well, Jim, ready to see the ship?"

9

Shotguns and Hand Grenades

THE *HISPANIOLA* WAS moored in the Upper Bay just beyond the mouth of the Kill Van Kull.

We went out to her in Mr. Blandly's steam tug, a stubby little boat with a tall black funnel. She was one of the last steam-driven boats in New York, Blandly told me as he let me take a turn at her big spoked steering wheel. The senator had brought his wad of invoices, but Blandly was too busy helping me steer to discuss them.

At last we were out in the bay and there lay the *Hispaniola*. She was big, with a high raked and flaring bow, a three-deck house that occupied her forward half, and a glassed-in wheelhouse. Booms and cranes angled up from her broad stern deck, and she had a thick businesslike smokestack just behind the wheelhouse, painted with a fresh blue stripe. Her sturdy hull was black and appeared, as we pulled closer, to be pocked with deep dents and gashes, though these were all painted over. She looked like what she was, Blandly assured me, a hardworking workboat, "with plenty of sea miles still under her keel."

I said I thought she was beautiful.

"The boy's got an eye for quality," Blandly announced, and suggested that if I studied hard in school, I should consider a career in naval architecture.

I asked why he had left the cannon on her foredeck. It

looked enormous and quite heavy and I wondered out loud whether the weight would affect her seaworthiness. I didn't know that much about ships, of course, but while the cannon lent a sort of dashing fighting-frigate air to the ship, it reminded me of the time I had seen my beloved Lyman with a fat man standing on her bow.

"The senator wanted to keep it," Blandly answered.

Dr. Livesey's face lighted up with one of her private smiles. "Boys will be boys."

"Might come in handy," the senator replied stiffly. "Besides, it would have cost a fortune to remove it."

"Right you are, sir," said Blandly, reaching over my head for a steering spoke. "Attaboy, Jim."

Soon we were close enough to hear her machinery running, and then alongside and up a little ladder from the steam tug to *Hispaniola*'s main deck. Senator Trelawney went first, reached down and hauled me up, then reached again for Dr. Livesey, who gave him her hand and bounded aboard like an excited collie.

Mr. Arrow, the chief mate, was waiting. He had a weatherbeaten face and black tattoos running up and down his scrawny arms. He greeted us with a nearsighted squint and I saw right away that he and the senator had become the best of friends. "It's a real pleasure, ma'am," he greeted Dr. Livesey. "And welcome aboard to you, young Jim. The senator promised we'd get along fine and I see he was right."

Things were a lot less friendly between the senator and the *Hispaniola*'s captain. A *lot* less friendly. We were looking over the main cabins where Dr. Livesey and the senator and I would sleep when Smollett appeared, glowering in the doorway. He was sharp-faced and scowling. He had piercing eyes that missed nothing, and he seemed habitually mad at everything and everybody on board.

He looked through me like I was a piece of furniture, and tossed Dr. Livesey a curt nod. The sight of Trelawney turned his already hard face grim. "We got problems, Senator."

"Now what?"

Smollett kicked the door shut behind him. Before he could speak, however, the senator introduced Dr. Livesey, who got another curt nod. As for me, the senator didn't waste his breath and I climbed up to the bunk Dr. Livesey had told me to take.

"All right, what's your beef, Captain?"

"Let me give it to you short and sweet, Senator. I don't like the voyage, I don't like the hands you hired. And I don't like my chief mate."

Senator Trelawney, as you've probably guessed by now, wasn't used to being spoken to that way, and he displayed one of his rare bursts of anger. "I suppose you don't like the ship either."

"I'll answer that at sea."

"How about your employer? What do you think of him?"

"Hold on," interrupted Dr. Livesey. "If the captain's got a problem I'd rather hear it now than a thousand miles offshore. But antagonizing him isn't going to help. You say you don't like the voyage, Captain. Can you tell us why not?"

Captain Smollett turned to Dr. Livesey and addressed her as if the senator had melted through the deck. "I was hired, ma'am, under what the senator called 'sealed orders.' Fine with me. Ready the ship and put out to sea and then find out where we're headed. Regular practice in wartime, but I figured he had his reasons. *Then* I find out the whole crew already knows exactly where we're going—every man but me. You call that fair? Makes me feel like a damned fool."

The senator muttered something, but Dr. Livesey shut him up with a look. "No, I don't call that fair. Then what?"

"Then I hear we're going for treasure. Hear it from my own deckhands. Now sailing for treasure is not exactly my favorite line of work. Gold—yeah, I know it's gold—has a way of driving normal men nuts. They figure they're going to get rich overnight, so screw orders. Every man for himself. Hell of a way to run a ship—especially a ship with a woman aboard, if you don't mind me saying, Doctor."

"I've worked with men," Dr. Livesey replied dryly. "I can handle it."

"Yeah, well, maybe you can—that don't change the fact that I'm going to have twenty crazy hands to keep in line. Bad enough a secret treasure hunt, but this here secret's been told to the parrot!"

"The crew have a parrot?" the senator asked.

Captain Smollett returned a stern look. "It's an expression, though as a matter of fact, Long John Silver just had one sent aboard. What I meant was it's been blabbed all over New York. And probably up and down the East Coast from Nova Scotia to Miami. Do I have to paint a picture for you, or can you understand that every wharf rat and gangster within three thousand miles is going to take a mighty close interest in where we're heading?"

"The senator and I have considered that possibility," Dr. Livesey admitted.

"Why do you think I left that cannon on the bow?" Senator Trelawney asked.

"If you fire more than six rounds with that cannon, the recoil will tear the ship apart. She wasn't built to be a warship."

"I think I know warships as well as you do, Smollett."

"Then you know that cannon'll peel the foredeck off like a can opener."

Dr. Livesey interceded again. "You said you don't like the crew, Captain. Can you tell us why? Are you saying they're bad seamen?"

"I'm saying I don't like them. And I'm saying I should have been allowed to choose my own men."

"You probably should have. My friend here should have

asked you to come along when he hired them. But I don't think he meant any harm by going ahead without you. But tell us, you don't like Mr. Arrow either?"

"Not one bit. He seems a competent seaman, but he's too palsy-walsy with the crew. A chief mate ought to stick to himself, not go drinking with the boys."

"Arrow drinks?" cried the senator, which earned him another stern look.

"It's an expression, sir. All I'm saying is a ship ain't a democracy."

"So what do you want us to do?" the doctor asked.

"Are you determined to go?" asked Captain Smollett.

"Absolutely," the senator fired back, and Dr. Livesey nodded.

"All right. Then get this: the men are stowing sawed-off shotguns in the fo'c'sle."

"What for?" asked the senator.

Even Dr. Livesey seemed shocked. "All of them?"

"All but one guy with a box of hand grenades."

"Well," said the senator. "Well . . . it's understandable, if what you say is true about everyone knowing why we're going—they probably figured they might have to defend themselves."

"Very likely," agreed Captain Smollett. "But, as I'm sure you remember in the navy, sir, it's customary to keep guns and crew apart until the captain orders weapons issued. So what I'm ordering, with your permission, sir, is all guns and hand grenades and any other explosives they've got their mitts on, be stowed with us in the main cabin. Including the shells for that damned cannon. Agreed?"

"Agreed," said the senator. "You're absolutely right . . . Anything else?"

"Oh, yes. Sir. You've brought some of your own men from home, I gather."

"Redruth, Joyce, and Hunter."

"Bunk them in the main cabin with us."

"Anything else?" Senator Trelawney asked through clenched teeth.

"One more thing. Loose lips sink ships—there's been too much blabbing."

"Way too much," the doctor agreed, but the senator was losing patience.

"You already registered that complaint, Captain."

Captain Smollett returned a cold sneer. "You have a map of an island. There's crosses on the map marking where the treasure is, and the island lies near—" He named longitude and latitude, only minutes and seconds from the exact location.

"I never told anybody that," yelled the senator, and turning to Dr. Livesey, "Janet, I didn't."

"Then how come the hands all know it?" Smollett asked grimly.

"Janet, did you? Jim?" He whirled on me. Watching quietly from the top berth, I shrank back, mutely shaking my head. I knew I hadn't but did he believe me?

"Neither did I," said Dr. Livesey, "but it doesn't matter now, does it?"

I had a strong feeling that neither she nor Captain Smollett believed the senator, but I must admit I did. I had seen enough of him to know he loved to talk, but I sensed something steady in him—I figured that Dr. Livesey would not have stayed friends with a total fool—and that steady thing would have stopped him from actually naming the island's coordinates.

"At any rate," continued the angry captain, "I don't know who has this map and I don't want to know. Don't tell me and don't tell Mr. Arrow, and anyone else aboard or ashore, or I quit."

The senator glowered at the threat, but something else was bothering Dr. Livesey. Her brow had furrowed and she got a thoughtful look in her eyes.

"Let me just sum this up a moment, Captain. You're saying you want us to keep the map a secret, and you want us to put only our friends in the main cabin, where you also want us to store every weapon on the ship. In other words, you're afraid of a mutiny."

"Don't put words in *my* mouth," retorted the captain. "I'm saying I'm responsible for this ship and as captain I intend to take the plain ordinary precautions any experienced mariner would. Arrow seems competent enough. I'm sure most of the men are honest and just looking out for their own defense. But defense is my job, Doctor, and I won't go to sea with an armed crew. No captain would."

Dr. Livesey smiled her warmest smile and Smollett, like Senator Trelawney or state trooper Sergeant Dance, turned agreeable. "Captain," she asked, "why do I have the feeling you came in here for another reason?"

"You get right down to it, don't you, Doctor? Fact is, I never expected the senator here to listen to a word I had to say. I figured he'd fire me or I'd resign."

"Fired," the senator assured him. "I would have chucked you overboard, if Dr. Livesey weren't here. Anyhow, I'll do what you want, though frankly I think you're a bit of a worrywart."

"Think what you like," the captain replied coldly. "You'll find I do my job." He spun on his heel, flung open the door, and stomped out.

"Sena*tor*," said the doctor, "sometimes you amaze me. You've managed to hire two of the most honest men in New York City—Captain Smollett and Long John Silver."

"Silver, for sure," said the senator. "But that stiff-necked pain in the butt is a sorry excuse for an American officer."

"We'll see," said the doctor.

Minutes later, sailors came trooping into the main cabin with stubby shotguns, some pistols, and the box of hand grenades. The arsenal included twenty shells for the bow cannon, wrapped in greasy paper and reeking of oil. Arrow and Captain Smollett watched over the transfer, then, ordering the men onto the stern deck, made a thorough search of the forward berths, uncovering a couple of shotguns apparently forgotten.

The surrender of the weapons was still underway when a launch came alongside with Long John Silver. The cook scrambled over the side like a cat. He had exchanged his walking stick for a crutch, for a reason that soon became apparent. "Where are you going with that?" he asked a sailor with a cannon shell.

"Guns and ammo to the main cabin."

"Kind of crowded in there already, ain't it?"

"My orders," said Captain Smollett. "Get supper started, Silver. Men'll need to eat."

"Aye, aye, sir," Silver saluted. "Soon as I shed my leg." With that he reached inside his trousers and unbuckled some straps. Then he grabbed his shoe like you or I would to take it off. But when he pulled, out from his trousers came a long, oddly white flesh-colored limb. "Hey, pal," he called to the launch pilot. "Take this to my wife."

And Silver tossed the leg over the side, leaped up with his crutch, and skipped toward the galley hatch. "Supper coming up," he cried, his empty pant leg flapping after him. He grinned back at me staring. "God forbid you'll ever need it, Jim, but if you do, you'll find a crutch holds better on a rolling deck. Just make sure she's got a rubber foot. Hey, Doc? Lend me a safety pin before I trip on my pants."

"That's a good man," said Dr. Livesey, heading to her cabin for a pin.

"Probably so," agreed Captain Smollett. "Hey! Boy!" I was gazing at the launch bearing Long John Silver's leg home to his wife. "Cabin boy! *You* I'm talking to. Get below and give the cook a hand."

As I fled his sudden wrath, I heard him tell Dr. Livesey,

"I don't care who brought him aboard, I won't have favorites on my ship."

At that moment I agreed totally with the senator. Captain Smollett was going to be a royal pain in the behind.

10

The Voyage

W E P R O V I S I O N E D A L L that afternoon and through the night, from lighters and barges that John Silver had commissioned to deliver food. It was a warm June night. The *Hispaniola* lay at anchor, still as a dock, so he told me to set up some barbecue grills on the stern deck, just outside the galley hatch, which I kept calling a door, and he kept patiently correcting until I got it right. He showed me how to mound the charcoal to start the fire and when the coals were glowing, he bounced out on his crutch, dragging a huge bucket of hot dogs and hamburgers, which we set sizzling. Soon the entire crew were sitting cross-legged on the deck, wolfing down the cookout and from that night on they all called John Silver "Barbecue."

Then the loading resumed, crates and boxes swung aboard by deck cranes. The bosun and chief engineer directed the stowage of deck and engine room supplies, and Long John and I scrambled to find space in the galley and the cook's hold. Captain Smollett was everywhere, and his cold eye saw everything. Once he waded in to a heap of crates, pointed at one and ordered, "Deep-six that." Senator Trelawney heard the splash and asked why. Smollett said, "Booze. Must have been delivered by mistake."

Moments later, he roared, "What the hell is this?" slapping a huge barrel, tall as me, which Long John had tied down on the stern deck in the shelter of the cabin. "Lashed in the lee of the house," he had translated to sea talk for my benefit.

"Pistachios, sir," Silver answered with the respectful salute he always threw the captain. "A treat for the hands. A sailor can scoop up a mittful if he wants a snack."

"I don't want to see shells littering the deck."

"I've already warned them about that, sir. First shell I see on deck, overboard the barrel."

Captain Smollett grumbled off to torment someone else, and Long John gave me a wink. But when I laughed, he cautioned me sternly. "Captain's got the lives of twenty-five souls to worry about, Jim. And even the mildest of master mariners are unhappy in port. He'll shape up once we're underway."

Thinking I would believe that of Smollett when I saw it, I avoided the captain and his eagle eye until dawn when he gave the order to up anchor. Despite a nap Long John had insisted I take around midnight, I was dead tired, having worked with him through the night. But I came wide awake when Senator Trelawney invited me up to the wheelhouse to watch us sail.

First light showed the ship's decks cleared at last, the cranes secured, hatches shut ("dogged down," John had taught me), and lines stowed. A hissing air windlass raised the anchor. The chain clanked up the hawsepipe and the anchor itself was drawn snug into the *Hispaniola*'s bow. Sailors hosed the mud off and the bosun signaled all secure to the wheelhouse.

"Think you can find the Narrows?" Captain Smollett growled at the helmsman. With that, he engaged the engine and seized the throttle in his huge hand. The diesel thundered. The *Hispaniola* shuddered into motion. I was so excited that I squeezed Dr. Livesey's hand. She threw her other arm around Senator Trelawney's shoulder: "We're off!"

Captain Smollett roared at Mr. Arrow that the ship looked "dirty as a garbage scow." Sailors grabbed huge gray mops and began furiously swabbing the decks. As we entered the Verrazano Narrows to slide between Brooklyn and Staten Island, the coxswain called out to Long John Silver, "Hey, Barbecue. Sing us a song!"

Silver's strong voice drifted up through the open wheelhouse windows, high and clear and piercingly audible over the murmur of the *Hispaniola*'s main engine:

> *"Oh, the monkeys have no tails,*
> *in Zamboanga."*

The words rocketed me back, of course, to the Admiral Benbow and the old captain pounding out the chorus on the bar. "The song! That's the captain's song."

"We all sang that song in the navy," said the senator.

"The navy stole it from the army," said Dr. Livesey, softly singing along with Silver. " 'Oh the moneys have no tails in Zamboanga. They were chewed off by the whales . . .' The army sang it in the Philippines. '. . . but before I'd serve again in Zamboanga, I'd rather serve a hitch in Hell.' Among it's politer lyrics."

The next minute the *Hispaniola*'s bow rose to a groundswell in the Lower Bay. Beyond the arms of Sandy Hook and Rockaway lay the broad Atlantic. Dr. Livesey tousled my hair, then clapped her hand over the senator's mouth—too late to muffle his cheer: "Treasure Island, here we come."

Thank God I wasn't seasick the first week of the voyage like the senator.

"They say," he muttered the morning he finally recovered, "that nothing is as bad as you imagine it will be. Take it from me, Jim, that's not true about seasickness."

I wasn't surprised I didn't get sick; when the carnival

came to town I never threw up on the rides like other kids. Besides, the sea was pretty calm most of the voyage, and the *Hispaniola*, while slow, turned out to be a steady ship. The crew were good seamen, and mean as he was, Captain Smollett obviously knew his business. So it would have been an easy two-week passage, except for several things that happened before we reached Treasure Island.

For one, Mr. Arrow turned out even worse than Captain Smollett had predicted. He had no respect from the sailors and they did as they pleased around him. Often, he seemed drunk, slurring his orders and stumbling around pie-eyed. Day after day Smollett would order him below, where Arrow would lie on his bunk staring at the ceiling, or get up and fall down and cut himself or blacken his eye and bruise his nose, which grew redder and redder as the ship forged south. Then he'd sober up for a couple of days and do a pretty good job, standing watch and navigating as a chief mate should.

Where he got his booze was a mystery. Smollett watched him like a hawk and twice had his cabin searched. Then, before we knew it, he was drunk again. When we asked him where he got it, he would laugh if he was drunk, and swear, when he was sober, that nothing stronger than coffee passed his lips.

Useless most of the time as a mate, and a bad example to the sailors, he was not mourned when one night he simply disappeared. Smollett had the ship searched stem to stern, but the mate was gone.

"Overboard," said the captain at lunch. "Saves me the trouble of tossing him in the brig."

There we were, a thousand miles at sea and short a chief mate. So one of the men had to be promoted. The bosun, Job Anderson, was the likeliest candidate. He kept his old title, but filled in as a sort of chief mate. Senator Trelawney stood watches too, as did the coxswain, Israel Hands, who'd sailed into every port from Marseilles to Shanghai.

Hands was pals with Long John Silver, which leads me to fill in a few more details I began learning about "Barbecue," our one-legged cook.

At sea, he carried his crutch by hanging it from a rope around his neck. This arrangement left his hands free. He used them like an acrobat, swinging his big frame around the galley as he fried potatoes, sliced vegetables, and butchered meat. On deck, in heavier weather, the sailors, who loved him and the treats he was always handing out, rigged grip lines for him. Hauling himself along them, he scrambled around quicker than I did with two legs.

The one he was missing was gone almost at the hip, and, after studying him sidelong for a while, I concluded that his "land leg," as he called his artificial limb, which neatly filled his pants ashore, would be a drag on a rolling deck. He had adapted as much as any man could to his loss, but the sailors who had sailed with him before pitied him, and struggled to explain to those who hadn't known him, what a man he had been.

"A cut above the rest," Coxswain Hands told me, as he crushed pistachio shells with his strong bony fingers. "Went to school, even had some college. He can talk like a professor when he feels like it. Brave as a lion, too: down in the South Pacific, I seen him lay out four Tonga knife-fighters with his bare hands."

As I've said, the crew respected and obeyed him. Sailors would stop by the galley in their free time for a smoke and a chat and often to ask advice. He kept the galley neat as a pin. There was always a pot of coffee on and usually a big iced chocolate cake or a cherry pie. To me he was always kind, always thanking me for my help—unlike Captain Smollett, who said nothing to me but *"Boy!"* at the top of his lungs. Somehow John had learned of my passion for Mounds Bars, for the ship had an inexhaustible supply. Similarly, Dr. Livesey never ran out of Gauloises, and the senator had an after-dinner cigar whenever he wanted.

Even Captain Smollett turned out to have a normal human desire—Fig Newtons, which appeared regularly as his dessert. Sometimes when I wasn't working I would finish a stroll around the ship and a gaze at the empty blue sea with a visit to the galley, where the pots were gleaming with polish and John's parrot was nattering to herself in her cage in the corner.

Silver would say, "Well, there you are, Jim. Come on in for a chat with old John. I bet you miss boys your own age, but let me try and fill in with a slab of that pie. Dig in, kid . . . Take a load off. Sit down and hear the news. I was just talking to my pal here, Captain Flint. I named my parrot after the meanest lowdown son of a bitch that ever sailed for reasons that will be obvious to anyone who spends time with the bird." (I had seen enough of "Captain Flint" not to argue that point.) "Captain Flint was just predicting a successful voyage."

And the parrot would screech, "Pieces of eight! Pieces of eight! Pieces of eight!" as loud as a fire siren until John either threw a dishcloth over her cage or threatened to include her in his next fish stew.

"Now that bird," John would say—pouring himself a fresh cup of java, as he called coffee, and cutting me another slice of pie—"is at least two hundred years old. They live mostly forever. You realize what that means, Jim? You know why she says 'Pieces of eight'? I'll tell you why and she'll confirm it. Two hundred years ago that bird sailed with pirates. Real pirates, Jim. Cutthroat buccaneers that terrorized the Spanish Main. That's the old name for the Caribbean, Jim, down where we appear to be headed. The Spanish Main. That bird has seen treasure with her own eyes. Real gold pieces of eight. And jewels and silver and all the riches the Spanish stole from the Indians, only to be stolen again by the pirates that old bird kept company with. You've smelled blood, haven't you, Captain?"

"Blood," said Captain Flint. "Blood, blood, blood, blood,

blood," until Long John threw a dishrag at her. He took a sip of his coffee and laughed. "After all the things she's witnessed, she must be bored out of her feathers sailing with the likes of you and me, eh, Jim?"

"Blood!"

"But you're my sweetheart, aren't you," and he would feed her a lump of sugar. For thanks the bird would curse a blue streak. "Ignore that," John would instruct me. "She don't know what she's saying—she's just hung out with the wrong crowd, and now she's too old a leopard to change her spots. Poor parrot, she can't help herself," he would say kindly. And before long, he had trained her to let me feed her pistachios.

But while I and everyone else on the ship thought the world of John Silver, the senator and Captain Smollett still bristled whenever they found themselves on the same deck. They were blunt men. The senator made it abundantly clear that he despised Smollett, while the *Hispaniola*'s captain never spoke a word unless spoken to, and then short and sharp and to the point, period. It made for some pretty uncomfortable meals, which fortunately I didn't have to sit at, though I was obliged to serve them up from John's galley. Of course with Smollett it wasn't just Senator Trelawney he hated. He hated everybody and everything on principle, except for Dr. Livesey, to whom he paid grudging respect. Only she could get him to admit that the crew wasn't as bad as he had feared and were actually performing their duties and behaving themselves.

"Good enough ship, but I don't like the voyage. If we were home tomorrow it wouldn't be too soon for me."

Only on the subject of the ship did he ever show any pleasure at all. "A real workhorse," he'd say. "A real lady the way she holds a course. I swear that boy could conn her singlehanded."

"Teach him," said Dr. Livesey, and my heart leapt.

"Too young."

Trelawney laughed. "Kid's too short to see over the spokes."

That was all Captain Smollett had to hear. "Boy," he growled. "Get up to the wheelhouse. Ask the cook for a milk crate to stand on and tell the bosun I said you should steer."

I raced to the galley, begged John Silver for a crate, and ran up the companionway to the wheelhouse.

I was having a ball at the wheel, standing on the crate John had given me, concentrating mightily on the compass, when the senator stomped into the wheelhouse muttering, "I swear I'd throw that son of a bitch overboard if we weren't already short of officers."

East of Cuba we hit some heavy weather. Seeing green water crash over the bow was a new and alarming experience. I couldn't help wondering, when the bow made like a submarine and the stern rose to the sky, whether the ship's powerful engine might not drive her right under.

But the *Hispaniola* took it in stride and Long John seemed unperturbed. We sailed in warmer and warmer waters with the happy crew sunning themselves lazily and partaking of his excellent meals and marvelous snacks.

"I've never liked a mollycoddled crew," Captain Smollett grumped to Dr. Livesey. "First thing you know they come to expect it and when they're disappointed there's the devil to pay. Mind you I'm not advocating a return to hardtack and flogging—though they had their adherents—but a little hardship toughens the hands and makes them pull as one. Look at them down there, munching pistachio nuts like there's no tomorrow."

But in fact, if it weren't for the barrel of pistachio nuts, there might not have been a tomorrow for any of us who were berthed in the main cabin with the guns and the treasure map. It happened like this:

By the end of the second week, we were closing in on the island. Smollett had calculated one day to landfall. The senator said twenty hours. By evening lookouts were standing on the monkey island, the railed deck atop the wheelhouse. We were heading SSW on a quiet sea. The wind was abeam and the *Hispaniola* was rolling steadily on the swell. A low-lying haze made it hard to see.

Just after sundown, when I had finished cleaning the galley and had paid my customary visit to the wheelhouse in hopes whoever was standing watch would let me steer a minute, I suddenly got hungry for a handful of pistachio nuts. So I swung down to the main deck. No one was there. Everyone was on the bow or the monkey island, sweeping the sea with binoculars, and cursing the fog.

Long John's pistachios had been a big hit and the barrel, which must have held a million of them, was nearly empty. I reached in, but the few left on the bottom were beyond me. I hoisted myself over the side, and leaning on my stomach, reached farther down. Just then the ship rolled a little harder than usual and upended me into the barrel, where I crunched down hard on my head. I saw stars and folded up like an empty bathrobe, too stunned for a moment to untangle my legs. When at last I did, I lay still, afraid that the slightest movement would make my head hurt even worse. Curled up in the dark, I started to gather my strength to climb out when I heard a heavy man sit down on the crate beside the barrel. It shook when he leaned against it and I was about to climb out and face his surprised laughter when the man began to speak. It was Silver's voice and before he had completed a sentence, I froze. Trembling, listening in terror, I realized that the lives of Senator Trelawney and Dr. Livesey and Captain Smollett depended on me alone.

11

What I Heard in the Pistachio Barrel

"FLINT WAS SALVAGE master," said Silver. "I was chief petty officer, thanks to this damned leg. The same kamikaze that blew it off blinded Pew."

He chuckled with amusement. "Dumb Jap died for his emperor never knowing we'd cut a deal to sell his admiral the exact position of where Halsey intended to land the marines. Bastard . . . We was running a big salvage tug for the navy—clearing harbors. 'Win some, lose some,' Flint always said. Easy for him. He got blown clear into the water without a scratch."

"I hear Flint was something else," said the man he was talking to, and I recognized the voice of the youngest sailor on the ship. He sounded excited and flattered that Long John trusted him with the confession that he had tried to betray our own troops. I guess that to him, like me, that war was a long time ago.

"Flint was loyal, I'll give him that," Silver agreed. "After the war when he launched the U-boat scam, first men he called were me and Blind Pew. I came out of that with ten grand and a promise of another shot at the bullion. Banked some of it. Bought my gin mill. Not bad for a swabbie up the hawsepipe, eh?"

"Not bad at all sir." (Back then, ten grand—ten thousand dollars—would buy a nice house, or five Cadillacs. So Silver and Pew had done not bad at all.)

"You see, kid, it's not earning that sets you up, it's saving. Where are the rest of Flint's guys now? Those that ain't drunk themselves to death or got picked up by the cops are living hand to mouth working for chumps' wages. Old Pew blew his ten grand in the first year we was on the beach, living it up like Rockefeller. Where is he now? Dead and buried, as it happens, but for the last couple of years he was rolling drunks for a living."

"So what's the use of money if you end up like that, Mr. Silver?"

"No use to fools, you better believe it. But look, you're young—a sharp kid, a real hotshot. I could tell the second I laid eyes on you. So let me give you some good advice, man to man. What you do with it is up to you, but I think you got the makings of a damned good ship's officer and a rich man besides."

If I had had a gun I would have "hotshot" him through the barrel. He was flattering the young sailor in the same words he'd tricked me with when Black Dog escaped from the Binocular Bar. Meanwhile he went on, completely unaware that I was listening.

"Here's the thing about guys who take chances. We live rough, and we run the risk of the gas chamber, but when the job is done, it's for a fortune instead of a measly paycheck. Trouble is, most of the money goes on booze and broads and before they know it they're taking chances again, which means the odds are stacking against them. Not me. I put mine into a decent business and let it earn more for me."

"Yeah, but if you do this thing you're talking about, you can't show your face in New York again. Every cop in Staten Island will be watching your bar."

Silver laughed at him. "What bar? By now my wife has sold the joint and moved the money to California. She'll be waiting under an orange tree for me—I would tell you the exact address, 'cause I trust you, only I don't want the other hands thinking I'm playing favorites."

"Do you trust your wife?" the young man asked boldly. His name was Dick. Even at my age I thought he was asking a very stupid question. Long John Silver, however, answered mildly, musing, "How should I put this . . . ? Let's say that people tend not to play fast or loose with John Silver. There were guys afraid of Pew, and even Pew as afraid of Flint, but Flint was afraid of me. You never saw a crew of hard cases like Flint had, but when I was their chief petty officer, they behaved like little *lambs* . . . Yeah, I trust my old lady, and anyone else who cuts a deal with me."

There was a pause, then Dick said, "Well, I'll cut a deal with you, sir. I wasn't sure about your offer, at first, but after our talk, let's shake."

They shook hands so hard that the barrel shook too. "Good kid," said Silver. "You're a real hotshot. Welcome aboard, hotshot. I knew all along you'd be one of the boys."

By now I had figured out most of Silver's terms. "One of the boys" and "taking chances" just meant gangsters, traitors, murderers—what when his parrot first sailed were called pirates. The little scene I had just overheard was him seducing one of the honest hands into joining his mob. Just then Silver gave a sharp whistle and I heard a third man stroll over and join them.

"Dick's all right," said Silver.

It was the coxswain, Israel Hands, who answered. "Figured he was no fool. Welcome aboard, Dick." Then he hawked and spat and said, "Okay, Barbecue, what I want to know is how long before we stop standing around with our dicks in our hands. When do we make our move? I've had it with Smollett. The bastard comes down on me like a ton of bricks. I want to feed him to the sharks, then I want a bottle, and a nice long visit with our lady doctor."

"Israel," replied Silver in a voice like gravel sliding down a chute. "Your head was never screwed on too tight, but at least you got ears. Big ears. So listen up. Get this and get it straight. If Captain Smollett so much as belches in your direction, you'll say, 'Yes sir, yes sir, three bags full.' You'll keep your trap shut. You'll stay sober. And you'll keep your mitts off the doctor till I give the orders. And son, you better memorize every word I just said."

"Okay, okay. I'm just asking when."

"When? I'll tell you when. Here's when. When I tell you when. And when's that gonna be? The last possible moment."

"Why wait?"

"Because we've got a first-class seaman, Captain Smollett, conning the ship for us, and the senator's men tending the diesel. Now the senator and his little doc-sie got Flint's map. I don't know where they hid it. Do you?"

"I'll get it out of her."

"Oh, I know you're an ace at interrogation, Israel, but why not use them to help us find the gold, first? What if you put the question to her, for instance, and it turns out he's hid half the map, but you've already shot him to frighten her? For instance. Why not, instead, allow them to find the gold and get it aboard, then we'll see when."

"That sounds like more waiting. Are you getting soft, John?"

I heard a thump. Then there was a gasp and a rattle as if someone were struggling to take a breath. A sound like *ack, ack, ack.*

"I think he's choking, sir," cried young Dick.

"Not yet," said Silver in a conversational voice. "Watch closely, Dick . . . You see him turning blue? Now, wait, you want to achieve a certain sky color before you let him go. Damn, the light has gone. Can't see—show you another time . . . Sit up, Israel . . . You get my point, pal?"

"*Ack!*"

"If I could trust you sons of bitches, I'd let them navigate us halfway home before I tossed them overboard."

"But we're seamen," protested Dick.

"Deckhands," said Silver. "We can steer a course, but what course?"

"We got one of them new radio direction finders," gasped Israel.

"And if it breaks, like the radar and the short wave already done, do you know anybody who can shoot the sun? In fact, do you know anybody who even knows which end of the sextant is up? Good Christ, Israel, the Caribbean's fifteen hundred miles across—fifteen hundred miles of unlit reefs. And what happens—Aw, the hell with it. Fact is I know we'll have to kill 'em before we leave the island, otherwise I'll have a mutiny on my hands. And by the time I put it down I'll have twenty-five corpses and have to sail the ship myself—so, goddamn you, we'll kill 'em on the island. Satisfied? You'll have your booze and your lady doc and probably end up in the gas chamber. Hurry, hurry, hurry."

Israel Hands kept trying to clear his throat. "You always been a sort of straight arrow, John. Most guys want to have a little fun along the way."

"And where are they now? Pew a beggar and dead. Flint's liver pickled in Savannah. A little fun along the way and where are they now? Could have retired like Texas millionaires if they'd only kept a lid on it."

"But when we take over?" asked Dick. "What do we do with them?"

"Dick, you're a man who gets right to the heart of the matter. Well, I'll tell you. Pew woulda just left 'em on the island to starve. Flint was more for chopping them into small pieces. Billy Bones, too. Though he preferred a forty-five slug in the brain."

" 'Dead men don't talk,' Billy used to say," Israel whispered. "Quick with a knife, of course, but when things called for a permanent solution, Billy put his faith in Mr. Colt."

"Yeah, Billy was something else. Shame you never met

him, Dick. I, on the other hand, am a little easier going, by comparison. An easygoing guy, I'm sure you've observed. But in this case, better safe than sorry, so I vote death too. When I'm sitting on the veranda watching my orange groves blossom, I don't want to see that crowd in the main cabin coming up the driveway with the sheriff. Wait, is what I say, but when the time is right, let her rip."

"Now you're talking," said Israel Hands.

"Don't worry about me, Israel. We're all in the same boat. I just ask one favor. Trelawney is mine. I'm looking forward to tearing his head off with my bare hands."

"As long as I can have the doctor."

Silver chuckled. "You were always one for the ladies— Dick, would you reach in the barrel and get me a handful of pistachios?"

I should have jumped out and run to the senator yelling for him to get the guns, but I was so scared I couldn't move a toe, much less my cramped legs. I heard Dick stand up. His hand descended into the barrel. Then another hand reached out and stopped him. "Screw the nuts," said Israel. "Let's have a drink."

"What the hell," said Silver. "Dick, just to show how much I trust you, pal, here's the key to my footlocker. Bring us a bottle."

That's where Mr. Arrow had got his booze.

While Dick was gone, Israel Hands whispered something I couldn't hear. Aloud, he said, "Dick's the last one. None of the rest'll join." So there were still a few honest seamen in the crew. But which ones?

Dick got back with the bottle and I could hear it glugging as they passed it around.

"Luck," said Dick.

Hands said reverently, "Here's to Captain Flint. I know he's down there someplace, grinning up at us."

Silver laughed. "Blood and gold. Can't have one without the other. Go together like Mom and apple pie."

Suddenly it got bright in the barrel. I thought they had trained the spotlight on me and ducked. But when I looked up, I saw that the moon had risen, silvering the diesel smoke that jetted from the stack. And then came a ragged chorus from the lookouts on the monkey island. *"Land! Land! Dead ahead!"*

12

Powwow

BOOTS AND BARE feet thundered on the deck as everybody ran to the bow. When the coast was clear, I jumped out of the barrel, snuck through the galley up to the main cabin, then forward on the weather deck, pretending I'd been asleep in my berth. Not that anyone noticed. By the time I arrived at the front of the ship, the entire crew had crowded into the vee of the *Hispaniola*'s bow. Dr. Livesey was hopping up and down straining to see over the broad shoulders. We helped each other climb onto the cannon and discovered that the belt of fog, which earlier had blinded the lookouts, had lifted with the moon.

We saw three mountains. They stood steep and sharp, ragged and angular in the moonlight. The two lower mountains were nearer to us and separated by a couple of miles. Behind them loomed the much taller third, so high that its peak was still lost in the fog.

I was in my own fog—a terror fog—still shaking from my session in the barrel. As if from another planet, I heard Captain Smollett bellowing orders. The *Hispaniola* came up a couple of degrees on a new course that would clear the island on the east.

"Okay," said the captain, once he was satisfied the helmsman wouldn't run us aground, "Any of you men know that island?"

Long John Silver swung forward boldly on his crutch. "I do, sir. A tramp I was cook on watered there. That's Treasure Island."

"Is that so? Was the anchorage on the south side, behind the little island?"

"You got it, sir. The little one is called Skeleton Island. Pirate hangout."

"Pirates! When was that?"

"Oh, centuries ago," Silver chuckled. "Back when my old parrot was born. One of the guys on the tramp knew the old sailing ship names they called it. Let me see . . . You see that low mountain to the north? That was Foremast Hill. Three mountains in a row from north to south. Fore, Main, and Mizzen."

I saw what Silver meant. It looked like a ship in the moonlight.

"But the Main, that's the big one with the cloud on it, they also called it Spyglass, because they kept a lookout there. Spyglass is the old pirate word for telescope, Jim."

"Have a look at this chart," said Smollett. "Is this the place?"

Long John practically tore the chart out of the captain's hand. But I could tell from the clean new paper that he was in for a disappointment. It was not the yellowed treasure map my mother and I had found in Billy Bones's duffel bag, but an exact copy, including everything—name, heights, and water depths—except for the red crosses and Captain Flint's notes. Without them, Long John could search those mountains for the rest of his life and never find a thing. For a split second he looked mad enough to strangle Smollett; instead, he hid his anger.

"Yes, sir. This is definitely it. Good-looking chart too, nicely drawn. Wonder who drew it? Here we go—'Captain Kidd's Anchorage.' That's what the guy on my ship called it. Look at this, they even got the current right. Strong around the south, then she swings north up the west coast.

Good move you went east. Especially if you want to enter the harbor."

Smollett took back the chart with a curt "Thank you, Cook. I'll call you when I need your help."

I was surprised Long John admitted he knew the island. And I got scared when I saw him coming my way. He couldn't possibly have known I was in the pistachio barrel, I told myself, but by now I was so frightened by his cruelty and his sneakiness that I jumped when he grabbed my arm.

"Lucky Jim," he said. "If Smollett takes us into that island you're going to have a ball. You'll go swimming, climb trees, hunt goats—yeah, there's goats on the island. You'll climb those mountains like a goat yourself. Makes me wish I were a kid again—almost forgot my leg a second there. Let me tell you, kid, it's a great island for the young with ten toes. Soon as you're ready to go exploring, you come to old John and he'll pack you a picnic lunch."

And he clapped me on the shoulder and hobbled back to the galley.

Captain Smollett, Senator Trelawney, and Dr. Livesey were talking together up on the bridge wing. I had to tell them what I'd heard in the barrel, but I was afraid somebody like Israel Hands, who was standing watch, would get suspicious if I just ran up to them and interrupted their conversation. Fortunately, Dr. Livesey spotted me pacing nervously on the weather deck and called me down, "Jim, sweetheart, run into the cabin and get me a pack of cigarettes, would you please?" Thanking God she was hooked on them, I brought her the cigarettes.

"Don't say anything," I whispered.

"What, Jim?"

"Shhh! Get the captain and Senator Trelawney down to the cabin, then call for me. I've got terrible news."

Surprise and alarm flicked across her face. Then she got hold of herself and said loudly, "Thanks for the smokes, Jim."

With that, she turned to the others and appeared to rejoin the conversation. They talked for a while. I watched from the edge of the wing, while pretending to study the dark shore we were slipping by. Neither of the men raised his voice or looked startled, but it was plain that she had filled them in on what I had told her. The next thing I heard was the captain calling for Job Anderson. A moment later came the order: *"All hands on deck."*

"Men!" said Captain Smollett. "Here's what's going on. That's the island we've been heading for. Senator Trelawney, who's a straight-shooter as you know, asked me how things were and I told him you guys have done a hell of a job. So he wants me and the Doctor to join him down in the main cabin to crack a bottle and drink your health and luck for the rest of the voyage, hoping the rest of the voyage'll go as well as we've come so far. And he wants rum served to you guys to drink *our* health. Pretty good deal, huh? How about a hand for the senator?"

They clapped and cheered loud and long. In fact, so loud and long I found it hard to believe they were planning to kill us.

"And one more cheer for Captain Smollett!" yelled Long John Silver. "A hell of a seaman!"

They cheered again.

At that, Smollett, the senator, and Dr. Livesey trooped below. A little later, the word came up to the bridge wing that Jim Hawkins was wanted in the cabin. Israel Hands gave a hoarse chuckle. "They're afraid you'll get drunk with the boys."

I ran down to the cabin, and found them sitting around the table with a bottle of wine. Dr. Livesey was chainlighting her next Gauloise from the last, a pretty good indication that she was upset, as she usually waited a few minutes between them. A porthole was open, for it was a warm night, and I could see the moonlight gleaming on Treasure Island's white sand beach.

"Okay, Jim," said the senator. "What's going on?"

I repeated Silver's conversation word for word. Nobody interrupted me, but they watched my face close as hawks and I could feel them thinking, How much do we believe a kid?

"Sit down, Jim," Dr. Livesey said when I was done. She gave me the chair next to her and poured me some Coke. Then, to my relief, they raised their glasses and toasted me, my luck, and my courage. I stared into my Coke. For some funny reason I felt tears coming into my eyes. I didn't know if it was just sheer relief from the fear of the last hour, or something deeper as if, in a way, I was no longer just a kid in their eyes.

"Captain," said Senator Trelawney, "you were right and I was wrong. I'm a first-class idiot and I'm ready for your orders."

"You're no more of an idiot than I am," the captain retorted. "I never in my life heard of a mutiny brewing in total secrecy. I can't believe I didn't realize what was going on. I might as well sign on as cabin boy and put Jim in command. This crew beats me."

"It's Silver," said the doctor. "The man's brilliant."

"I'd like to see him lit up brilliant in the electric chair," replied Smollett. "But just talking about it won't help. We've got to do something. We all know we're going to have a fight on our hands. I say hit them before they hit us, when they least expect it . . . Now I see three or four points. If it's okay with the senator, I'll just lay 'em out."

"You're the captain," Senator Trelawney said grandly. "Let's hear them."

"First, we have to go on, because we can't turn back. If I give the order to turn around, we're dead. Second, we have a little time, at least until we find the gold. Third, some of the men are still on our side. Can we count on your men, Senator?"

"Absolutely. That's three. Ourselves make seven, counting Jim and you, Doctor. How about the crew? Who's still honest?"

"Most likely those that the senator hired," said Dr. Livesey. "The ones he signed up before Silver came along."

" 'Fraid not." The Senator dashed that hope. "Israel Hands was one of mine."

"I trusted Hands too," admitted the captain.

"I can't believe these sons of bitches are Americans," the senator exploded. "I'd like to sink the ship with them in it."

"Problem is," said Captain Smollett, "we can't start a fight till we know who's on our side. We're just going to have to hang in here and keep a sharp eye. Lay low until we figure out who we can trust. Which is tough. I'd rather fight now and end it one way or another."

"What about the radio?" asked Dr. Livesey. "Still broken?"

"Deader than the radar," the captain answered gloomily. "Between those two modern marvels we don't have enough spare parts to make a coat hanger. I'll bet those scum poured a bucket of seawater into the radio, just to make sure we couldn't call for help. Not that it was much of a radio to begin with."

Out of habit, Senator Trelawney began to defend the army surplus radio Mr. Blandly had picked up cheap, but the doctor cut him off, saying, "Jim's our best chance at finding out who's on our side."

"How's that?"

"The men are used to him hanging around. They think he's just a kid. Maybe they'll let something slip."

Senator Trelawney turned to me, hope in his eyes. "Doc is right. We're counting on you, Jim."

"Be careful," warned Captain Smollett. "They'd slit a spy's throat soon as look at him."

I wanted to crawl under the table. I couldn't see how I could get Silver's men to tell me any of their secrets. And in the meantime we could talk ourselves blue in the face, but the fact was there were only seven out of twenty-six aboard the *Hispaniola* we could count on in a knock-down, drag-out fight to the death. And of these seven, there was me, a boy, and the doctor, a woman. So that the grown men on our side were five to Silver's nineteen.

PART THREE

MY SHORE
ADVENTURE

13

How I Got Ashore

TREASURE ISLAND LOOKED a lot different in daylight.

We were close when I came out on deck the next morning. The *Hispaniola* had stopped and was rolling wildly on a heavy swell, just a half-mile southeast of the low eastern shore. I could see grayish-colored woods covering most of it. Here and there was a glimpse of yellow sand, or the dark green of a couple of pine trees, but the island was mostly a sad-looking gray.

The hills rose higher than the trees in tall gloomy towers of bare rock. Each was oddly shaped, but Spyglass looked the strangest; it was three or four hundred feet higher than the others with sides as straight up and down as the skyscrapers I'd seen in New York and chopped off square at the top like a pedestal you could put a statue on.

Our ship was heaving on the ocean swell, creaking, groaning, and banging around while the senator's men worked down in the engine room trying to lubricate an overheated tail-shaft bearing. I couldn't take a step without hanging on to the handrails and I began to feel woozy. As I've said, I didn't get sick at sea, even in the worst storms. But this carnival sitting and rolling in one spot was more than I could take, especially on an empty stomach, and if it went on much longer I knew I'd join the senator leaning over the side.

You'd think I'd have been glad to see land after all this time at sea, especially on such a sunny bright day, with the birds diving for fish and filling the air with their excited cries, but in fact I felt awful. We had come a long way to find a grim and creepy place. Maybe it was the seasickness coming on, or maybe the sad gray woods ashore, or the surf we could hear thundering ominously onto the narrow beach, or maybe the harsh stony mountains; whatever, my heart was sinking and I hated the sight and the very thought of Treasure Island.

With the abysmal swell threatening to drive the ship onto the rocks, and the propeller still frozen while Joyce, Hunter, and Redruth labored frantically below, it looked like we had already seen the best part of the day. Captain Smollett confirmed that, ordering the boats to be launched into the heavy swells to tow the ship around the island. The men didn't like it. This was heavy work even in calm seas. But with the sun blazing down and no wind to cool us even as the swell banged the boats against the hull and tossed their crews like ping-pong balls, it was sheer hell. I had volunteered for the lead boat—though I was too light to be of any help and mostly got in the way as the men struggled with the tow line. Anderson was in command of my boat, but instead of maintaining order and telling the hands what to do, he grumbled as loud as the rest of them.

Swearing loudly as we finally got the line paid out and began pulling the heavy ship in earnest, he said, "Three-four miles of this crap and we'll be out of it." The others cursed and complained and I could see that we were going to have serious problems very soon. One look at the island and these guys were ready to forget who was boss.

Slowly the two launches dragged the *Hispaniola* the miles around the corner of the island and into the mouth of the inlet protected by Skeleton Island. At that point the senator's men finally got the tail shaft turning again, so we climbed back aboard and streamed the boats astern as the ship headed in under her own power.

Long John Silver conned the ship. Perched beside the helmsman on leg and crutch, it was pretty clear he knew the channel like the back of his hand, knew it even better than the chart. We had a man in the bow throwing the lead—the sonar depth finder having joined the radar and the radio on the electronic scrap heap—and every time he called the depth it was deeper water than the chart promised. Long John never even hesitated, explaining to me, hovering by his elbow, "The ebb tide scours the channel better than a dredge."

We continued up the inlet into an anchorage. Dead center between Skeleton Island and the main island—a third of a mile from either shore—Captain Smollett ordered, "Let go the anchor!"

The crew screwed up and he started yelling. The chain jammed in its locker. They had to disconnect the anchor and bend on a big rope instead. Finally the heavy iron flukes splashed into the still water and dropped many feet to the clean white sand below. The splash scared thousands of birds flying over the woods. But they settled down quickly and when Captain Smollett ordered "Stop engine!" the harbor was suddenly quiet as death.

It was virtually landlocked. We might as well have set the ship down in a pond. Woods covered the flat shore on all sides. In the distance, the mountains looked down on us as if we were on the stage of a theater. Into our pond flowed a couple of rivers—swamps, actually. The foliage surrounding them was a bright poisonous green. We couldn't see the house or the old bunker and if we didn't know they were on the chart, we might have thought we were the first human beings ever to stop at the island.

The air was heavy and dead still. A faint muttering noise in the distance was the surf, half a mile away, beating at the mouth of the inlet. A stagnant smell hung in the air—the stink of rotting leaves and dead trees. Dr. Livesey wrinkled her nose. "There may be gold," she muttered quietly, "but dollars to doughnuts there's damned sure malaria. Told you you'd thank me for those shots, Jim. Captain Smollett, I suggest you remind all hands to take their quinine."

Smollett's order was met with open jeers.

Since climbing back aboard the ship from the boats the crew had been lolling around the deck like they were on a picnic and virtually ignoring orders. They had laughed as they screwed up dropping anchor, and now were eying the island like they were heading for a party. I walked around the deck and had the strong feeling that they were about one inch from mutiny. I murmured this impression to Dr. Livesey, who passed it on to the senator and Captain Smollett.

"Look!" said the doctor.

Long John Silver was limping from group to group, trying to reason with them. Orders came down to let more scope in the anchor line, and he was up in a flash with a smiling "Aye, aye, sir," urging his fellow pirates to lend a hand. He led them by example and, when the job was done, sang a few verses of "The Monkeys." Just as I had heard in the barrel, the cook was as worried as we were, though for vastly different reasons.

The captain called another meeting in the cabin.

"It's about to blow," he warned. "Next order I give they'll try to shove down my throat. If I tough it out, they'll pull knives. If I back down, Silver will realize we suspect and then we'll see knives."

"So what do we do?" The senator looked really worried.

"I hate to say it, but Silver's our only chance. He's as anxious as we are to keep order, at least till we've found the gold. Until then, he is our friend and he'll do whatever it takes to knock sense into those scum . . . Tell you what. I'm going to suggest shore leave."

"Shore leave?"

"Let them go ashore, blow off some steam, and give Silver a chance to have some time alone with them. If they all go, we up-anchor and blow this joint. If they only leave a few aboard, maybe we can take 'em. If none of them go, then we've got a problem. Fortunately we've got the firepower here in the cabin."

He inserted a key in the gun locker, while the senator went out and got Redruth, Hunter, and Joyce. They didn't seem all that surprised by our news and took the pistols offered. Redruth and Hunter, at least, checked them over like men who knew weapons. Dr. Livesey lingered over a .45 automatic, but settled instead on a neat little .32 police special, which she tucked into her blouse. Captain Smollett shoved a few guns in his big pockets and marched out to deal with the crew.

"Now hear this, you guys. It's been a helluva hot day and a lot of backbreaking work, so I'm ordering shore leave!"

They cheered like the Fourth of July, and before the roar subsided I heard Senator Trelawney mutter to Dr. Livesey, "Silly bastards think they'll trip over the gold when they hit the beach."

"Cook," cried Captain Smollett. "Rustle up a heap of sandwiches and plenty of cold lemonade. Take the launches. I'll give a hoot on the whistle right before sundown to come back. Have fun, boys. You earned it."

Another cheer sent the birds flying around the anchorage again, squawking like banshees. Smollett ducked back into the cabin, which was a good move, I thought, because if he had stayed on deck it would have been clear to everyone that he had to be aware of the real situation. The fact was written plain as day on every hard-bitten face that Long John Silver, not Smollett, was the real captain of the crew. Not that Long John wouldn't have his work cut out for him; like the impatient Israel Hands I'd overheard from the barrel, they were itching to fight even Long John for a shot at the gold. The honest sailors—and it turned out we had a few aboard—must have been pretty dumb not to notice. More likely they just let the ringleaders take over, but wouldn't follow them any farther than this. It was one thing to stand around bitching with your hands in your pockets, quite another to seize the ship and kill a bunch of innocent people.

Soon the shore party was assembled. Six men stayed aboard. The remaining thirteen, including Silver, climbed into the boats and prepared to cast off.

It was then that I got the first of several crazy ideas that helped keep us alive. There was no way we could take the ship from the six left behind before the others came screaming back to help them. So with no fight in the offing, my friends didn't need me. Without thinking much about it, I decided to go ashore with the main crew. They were busy pushing off from the hull, so I just rolled over the bulwark and plopped into the bow of the nearest launch. I hunched down out of the way as they shoved off. Only one man noticed.

"That you, Jim? Jeez, duck down, kid. Don't let Long John see you."

But Silver, in the other boat, heard. He looked over sharply. "Is Jim Hawkins in that boat?"

A few mumbled I was, and I immediately realized I'd made a bad mistake.

The launches raced to the beach, engines roaring, the men singing and cheering with their mouths full of sandwiches. My boat had a head start and a bigger engine and we shot ahead. The helmsman ran the bow in between two trees, while Long John's boat was still a hundred yards behind. I caught a branch, swung onto dry ground, and hit it running as Silver roared, "Jim! Jim, wait up!"

You will not be surprised that I didn't obey. Jumping, dodging tree trunks, ducking limbs, I ran and ran and ran until I could run no farther, and collapsed facedown in the sand, gasping for breath.

14

First Blood

WHEN I FINALLY caught my breath I saw that I had crossed a marshy area full of willows, reeds, and weird swampy trees. I had come out on the edge of an open stretch of rolling sandy ground, about a mile long, dotted with some pines and a great number of contorted trees, growing a little like oaks, but with leaves as pale as weeping willows. Across the open ground stood one of the hills, with two craggy peaks shining brightly in the sun.

Here and there bloomed flowers I didn't recognize. Here and there, snakes sunned. One of them raised his head from a rocky ledge and hissed at me; or rather, rattled. Coming from Long Island, I had never seen a rattlesnake, but I had seen plenty of westerns. I walked carefully around him, keeping my eyes peeled for his friends.

I came to a long dense clump of those oaklike trees—live, or evergreen, oaks, I found out later—which grew low along the sand like thorn bushes, their branches twisted, their leaves compact as blueberry. The dense clump extended down from the top of one of the sandy knolls, spreading wider and growing taller until it reached the edge of the broad reedy marsh, through which the nearest of the little rivers flowed toward the anchorage. The marsh steamed in the strong sun, making the outline of Spyglass shiver like a mirage.

Suddenly there was movement in the reeds. A duck flew up, quacking. Another followed, and in seconds a giant cloud of birds erupted from the marsh, circling and screaming. I took it as a warning that my shipmates were approaching the marsh and within seconds heard that I was right. A voice, low and distant, grew louder and nearer.

Frightened, I dove under a live oak and crouched there, afraid to even breathe.

Another voice answered, and then the first voice, which I recognized as Silver's, rumbled again and went on rumbling for a long time, insistent, demanding, only now and then interrupted by the others. It sounded to me like they were discussing something very seriously, almost fiercely, but I couldn't hear their words.

At last they fell silent and seemed to sit down. They didn't get any nearer and the birds landed again in the swamp.

I began to feel guilty that I wasn't doing my job. If I'd been dumb enough to go ashore, the least I owed my friends was to listen in on Long John Silver's plans. Which unfortunately meant sneaking closer through the trees. Much closer.

I could tell exactly where he was, not only by the sound of his voice and the voice of the man he was talking to, but also by the fact that right over their heads some birds still flew and squawked, long after the majority had landed.

Crawling on hands and knees, I headed slowly toward them, painfully aware that if they spotted me I was a goner, for there was no way I could get out of the thick brush before the two men headed me off. At last, raising my head above the leaves, I could see them in a little clearing beside the marsh, Long John Silver and Tom a crewman, talking face to face.

The sun beat down on them. Silver had tossed his hat aside and his big, broad, open face, gleaming with perspiration, was lifted to the crewman's as if he were begging him to see reason.

"Listen, pal. It's because I think the world of you. You're tops in my book. If you weren't, you think I'd be trying to protect you? It's all over, man. They're going ahead, with or without us. Jesus, if any of those crazies heard me trying to warn you, they'd mail our bones home—mine too, pal. Not just yours. I'm going way out on a limb for you."

"Silver," said Tom—and I could see he was not only red in the face, but struggling to control his hoarse, shaking voice—"Silver, you're old and you're honest, they say, and you've got plenty of dough stashed in that gin mill of yours, which a working stiff like me don't have; and you're brave—or I miss my bet. So will you tell me how you, of all people, could get mixed up with that mob? You're not their kind of guy. And as far as I'm concerned, I'd sell my right hand before I'd throw in with that scum. If they was to mutiny—"

All of a sudden he was interrupted by a noise. I had just heard the words of one of the honest hands—and here came news of another, from far out in the marsh: an angry yell, a shout, and then a terrible scream.

Spyglass Mountain echoed the long-drawn-out horrid sound, again, again, and again. The marsh birds shrilled into the sky like a dark cloud. The death yell was still ringing in my brain when the marsh grew quiet again and the birds fluttered down, and only their rustling wings and the distant booming of the surf disturbed the thick heat of the afternoon.

Tom had jumped at the scream, looking wildly about for its source, but Silver didn't bat an eye. He just stood resting lightly on his crutch, watching the honest Tom like a coiled snake.

"John!" cried Tom, reaching out his hand.

"Hands off!" cried Silver, leaping back nimbly.

Tom looked shocked and angry. "Hands off? What, do you got a guilty conscience? What in the hell was that scream?"

"Scream?" Silver smiled back, even warier than before, his eyes as hard and narrow as bunker slits. "Scream? Probably Alan."

Tom turned out to be a hero.

"Alan? There's a shipmate to be proud of. As for you, John Silver, you son of a bitch, we've been buddies a long time, but I ain't hanging around with you no more. If I die, at least I'll die honest. You've killed Alan? Kill me too, if you can."

Bravely, he turned his back on the cook and headed for the beach. But he didn't get far. With a yell, John grabbed ahold of a tree branch and, balancing himself on it, whipped the crutch out of his armpit and threw it. The point struck poor Tom hard between the shoulder blades. His hands flew up as if he'd been speared; he gave a sort of gasp, and fell on his face.

I couldn't tell how badly he'd been hurt, though by the sound of impact the crutch might have broken his spine. Whatever, he didn't have a chance when Long John Silver drew his knife. Agile as a monkey, even without a leg or his crutch, the cook was on top of him in a flash, twice burying his blade up to the hilt in his defenseless body. Hidden in the brush, I could hear him grunt as he struck the blows.

I started to lose it. The whole island swam in huge, lazy, misty circles—Silver, the birds, Spyglass—round and round and round, while all sorts of bells seemed to ring and distant voices shouted in my ear.

When I came to, the murderer had straightened himself out. He had his crutch under his arm again and his hat on his head. At his feet lay Tom's body, utterly still. Oddly, nothing else had changed. The sun still burned down on the steamy marsh and the tall mountain, and I could hardly believe that I had just seen a man murdered before my eyes.

Silver bent down and wiped his bloody knife on the grass. Then he pulled a whistle from his pocket and blew several blasts. I didn't know the meaning of the signal traveling through the hot humid air, but I knew to be scared. More men would come. What if one of them spotted me? They had just killed two honest men who refused to join them. After Tom and Alan, I'd be next.

Quietly I turned around in the bush and crawled away as fast as I could without making too much noise. As I headed for the woods, I could hear John's crew calling back and forth, a sound that doubled my speed. When I got out of the live oaks, I ran like a fiend, not caring about direction, frantic to put distance between me and them as my fear exploded into a mindless, hopeless frenzy.

It was hopeless. When Captain Smollett fired the gun to come back to the ship, how could I go down to the launches? John's men would break my neck the second they saw me. They'd see the fact that I'd run away as proof I knew too much. It was all over. I was cut off from the *Hispaniola;* cut off from the senator and Captain Smollett; cut off from Dr. Livesey. I had only two choices: hide until I starved to death; or quicker death on the blade of Silver's knife.

Thinking all this only made me run faster. Before I noticed my route, I found myself at the foot of the little hill with two peaks, on a part of the island where the live oaks grew taller and farther apart, more like forest trees. Among them were scattered tall pines, fifty or seventy feet high, and the air smelled fresh, cooler than down at the swamp, almost crisp by comparison.

And here something new to fear stopped me dead in my tracks, with a pounding heart.

15

The Man of Treasure Island

I WAS SCRAMBLING alongside a steep, stony hill when a bunch of gravel fell rattling through the trees. I looked up and saw a large figure jump behind the trunk of a pine. I couldn't tell if it was a bear or a man or a monkey, only that it was large, dark, and shaggy. Frightened, I skidded to a stop.

Now I was cut off on both sides—Long John Silver and his killers behind me, this scary thing lurking in the woods ahead. I hesitated only a second, instantly realizing that I preferred the danger I knew to the unknown. Silver's gang, even Long John himself, seemed less frightening than this thing in the woods. I turned around, slowly so as not to provoke it; then, shooting nervous glances over my shoulder, I headed back toward the boats.

As I did, the thing moved from behind its tree and swiftly circled ahead to cut me off. I was tired from running, but even if I'd been completely rested, there was no way I could cover ground with the speed with which it flitted from tree to tree. Fast as a deer, the creature ran like a man on two legs, but not like any man I had ever seen, stooping almost double, hunkered low to the forest floor. Still, I began to realize, it was definitely a man.

I remembered the sailors saying that the old Carib Indians, which the Caribbean was named for, were cannibals. I took a deep breath to scream for help. But at the same time, the fact that the creature bearing down on me was a man meant he just might not be as dangerous as Long John Silver. Looking around for some way to escape, I suddenly remembered the little pistol the senator had issued me in the cabin. So, realizing I wasn't completely defenseless, I walked boldly toward the man of the island.

He had disappeared behind another tree trunk, but he must have been watching, because when he saw me heading in his direction, he stepped out to meet me. Then he hesitated, stepped back, came ahead again, and then, to my amazement, suddenly threw himself down on his knees and clasped his hands in prayer.

I stopped. "Who are you?"

"Ben Gunn," he answered in a voice as hoarse and creaking as a rusty hinge. "I'm poor Ben Gunn. I haven't talked to another human being in three years."

I could see he was no Indian. His skin was deeply sunburnt. Even his lips were black. But his eyes were as blue as mine. I had never seen anyone as raggedly dressed. His clothes seemed to be made of ripped canvas and ragged strips of oilcloth. They were nothing more than patches upon patches held together by bits and pieces of brass buttons, rusty zippers, and loops of rawhide. The only solid piece in his whole outfit was a leather belt around his waist, with a tarnished brass buckle. Next to Ben Gunn, Old Billy Bones, "the Captain," would have looked like a clothes model in the Sears Roebuck catalog.

"Three years?" I exclaimed. "Were you shipwrecked?"

"Left behind," he said sadly. "Three years I've lived on goats and berries and oysters. I didn't take it lying down. No way I was going to sit around to wait to die. But, God, I've missed real food. Hey, pal, you wouldn't by any chance have a Fig Newton on you, would you? No. Jesus, the nights I've dreamed I found a box of Fig Newtons, then woke up and found myself still stuck here . . ."

"If I ever get aboard again," I said, "we've got tons of them on the ship."

He had been staring at me sort of goofily as we talked, feeling my jacket and acting thrilled to be with another human being. But when I mentioned the ship, his face lighted. "Ship? What do you mean if you ever get aboard? Who's to stop you?"

"Not you, I'm sure."

"Dollars to doughnuts on that, kid. Say, what's your name?"

"Jim."

"Jim, Jim," he repeated, rolling it happily on his tongue. "Well, Jim, in case you don't know it, you're looking at a guy who's lived like an animal, a guy who's been about as bad as bad can be. Looking at me now, you wouldn't think, Hey, here's a guy who grew up in a good home. Would you?"

"Well, now that you mention it, no."

"Fact is, I did. I had a fine mother, who raised me properly. I could rattle off the Pledge of Allegiance faster than any kid in school and I knew every verse of 'The Star Spangled Banner.' Then it all went to hell. Started innocently enough, I thought, pitching pennies on the street corner. Then I smoked a cigarette and drank a beer. My mother warned me—predicted every one of my steps into the gutter, God rest her good soul—but I didn't listen. So in a funny way, God gave me a lucky break—one last chance—sticking me here on this island. I've had plenty of time to think it over. Best thing that ever happened to me. I'm back on the straight and narrow. You won't catch me drinking rum ever again—except for a little snort to celebrate my good luck getting rescued, of course, the second I can get my hands on some. I swear I'll be good and I know how. And Jim"—he looked around warily, lowered his voice, and whispered in my ear—"I'm also rich."

I figured the poor man had flipped his lid, living alone so

long. It must have shone on my face, because he shouted his crazy claim again. "Rich! Rich, I tell you. And I'll make you rich too. You'll thank your lucky stars you found me."

But suddenly his face darkened. He gripped my arm and shook a threatening finger.

"The truth, Jim. Tell me the truth. That ship of yours ain't Flint's ship, is it?"

I almost cheered out loud. I'd found a friend, at last, in this crazy castaway. "No. It's not Flint's ship. Flint is dead. But the problem is, some of Flint's old crew are aboard and they've started to mutiny. Already killed two men who wouldn't go along with them."

"Is one of them a man—with one—leg?" he gasped.

"Silver?"

"Oh, Jesus. Silver."

"He's the cook. And their ringleader."

Gunn was still holding my arm, and at that he jerked it hard. "If you were sent by Long John, I'm a dead man . . . What's your part in this, Jim? Spill it, kid. Whose side are you on?"

I decided immediately to tell him the whole story, starting at the day the old sailor turned up at my parents' hotel, right down to the present moment. Gunn listened closely and when I was through, patted me on the head.

"Good kid. But you're in a jam, aren't you? Okay, put yourself in Ben Gunn's hands and maybe things'll work out. Ben Gunn's the guy for you . . . and your pals. Tell me, this senator, would he show his gratitude if I helped him out of a jam too?"

I told him that Senator Trelawney had always been very generous to me.

"Yeah, well, I'm not talking about him offering me a job mowing his grass. I got no interest in a job mowing his grass. I mean, would he cut me in for maybe a hundred grand, out of money that's almost mine already?"

"I'm sure he would. The deal was, everybody would share."

"*And* a ride home?" A shrewd expression lighted his sun-blacked face.

"Sure he would. Besides, once we get rid of Silver's gang, we'll be short-handed running the ship."

"Wonderful." He breathed a sigh of relief. "Wonderful. He's a gentleman and he'd need my help. Wonderful . . . Okay, Jim," he went on. "Here's my deal. Here's what I'll tell you, and no more. I was on Flint's ship when he buried the treasure we salvaged from the Nazi sub."

"You mean it?"

"No joke, kid," said Ben Gunn. "Flint took six men ashore—that many strong men to carry it. They stayed ashore a week, while we stood off the coast, rollin' our guts out. Then, one day, he signaled us to come in close. And out he came all alone in a little boat. He had a bloody bandage on his head and his face was white as bone. But he made it out, while the other six were left behind, dead and buried. Nobody on the ship could figure out how he pulled it off, but it was blood and guts—one against six—and Flint won. Billy Bones was the mate, Long John the chief. They asked Flint where the gold was. Flint looked them right in the eye and laughed. 'Go look if you want, but the ship's going back for more.' You see, Flint intended to resume the salvage. But we never did get back to the sub. Ended up in Savannah, for some damned reason I could never figure out.

"Well, three years ago I was on another ship and we spotted this island. I said, 'Boys, Flint buried the Nazi gold here. Let's look for it.' The captain didn't like it, but the whole crew came over to me and we hit the beach. Twelve days we searched and every day the crew got madder and madder. Finally, they said Screw this, and headed back to the ship. Only they were so mad at me, they left me standing in the surf. I begged them not to leave me. They threw me a pick and shovel and told me to have fun. Then they tossed me a gun with one bullet. 'In case you get bored,' they yelled. Big joke, eh, Jim?—Three years, my boy. Three long years. Not a bite of decent food, not a burger, not a malt. Just goat, oysters, and berries. But look at me. Do I look like a dumb swabbie? No, you say, and I say, 'Well, I weren't no dumb swabbie.' "

He winked and slapped my back.

"So you just fill your senator in on what's happening and who I am. You tell him I spent three years alone here and sometimes I'd pray and sometimes I'd think about my dear old mother, but mostly I had business to keep me busy. Then you give him a wink and he'll know what we're talking about. Eh? Eh?"

And he winked again like we had a big secret.

"Then you'll say to the senator, 'Gunn's a damned good man and he'd rather deal with an honest gent of a senator than a pack of gangsters, having been one of them himself, back before he remembered the difference between right and wrong while traipsing around this island doing that thing I was talking about earlier."

"I don't know what you're talking about," I said. "But it doesn't matter, since I can't get back to the ship to tell the senator anything anyhow."

"Hmm. That's a problem, all right. Well . . . There's always the little boat I made with my own two hands. Stashed under a white rock. Worse comes to worst, maybe you and I can take her out tonight, after dark—Hey! What the hell is that?"

"That" was the thunder of cannon fire—echoing from the mountains and bellowing from one end of the island to the other.

"They started fighting!" I yelled. "Come on!"

I began running toward the harbor, no longer afraid of anything, while Ben Gunn loped beside me, keeping pace as easily as if he had wings.

"Left!" he said. "Left. Bear left, Jim. Head under the

trees—see there, there's where I killed my first goat. They hide up in the hills now. They're scared of Ben Gunn. Hey, there's the cetemery."—cemetery, he must have meant—"See them mounds? That's where them six sailors I told you about lay.—'The worms crawl in, the worms crawl out.'—Sometimes I come by and pray for 'em. You know, if it felt like a Sunday. I know it's not a church, no preacher, but hell, it's the thought that counts, right?"

I kept running. So he babbled on and didn't seem to notice that I never answered.

After a while the cannon was answered by a long volley of small-arms fire crackling as if a dry brush pile had burst into flame. Then it died down. I ran harder until, a quarter mile ahead, I saw the American flag flying in the air above a clump of trees.

PART FOUR

THE STOCKADE

16

Narrative Continued by the Doctor; How We Abandoned Ship

THE CAPTAIN, MY senator, and I were talking things over in the cabin when the launches shoved off with the men on shore leave. We could hear them bellowing "Oh, the monkeys have no tails in Zamboanga," a song that would always remind me of the war and bars I should have stayed out of.

The big question was could we overpower the six they'd left behind and up-anchor before the rest came screaming back to stop us. Smollett and I voted to take the chance, and I was working on the senator, when Hunter crashed in to the cabin with the news that Jim had sneaked into one of the boats going ashore.

"That little son of a—Whose side is he on?"

"We asked him to spy," Smollett said gravely. "That's what he's doing."

I had an awful vision of returning his body to Jim's mother. The way the crew were acting I knew we'd never see him alive again. I ran out on deck, the men trailing after me. The harbor stunk like a hellish brew of malaria and dysentery. Tar seam-caulking stuck to our shoes and it was hotter than ever.

The wiseguys who had stayed aboard were sitting and complaining in the shade of a tarp they'd rigged over the foredeck. Ashore, we could see the launches tied to trees

and a man guarding each, next to where the river flowed out
of the swamp. One of them was still whistling "The Monkeys."

There was no way we could run for it with Jim in Silver's
clutches. But we couldn't just wait around, so we decided
that Hunter and I would row ashore in the dinghy to see
what was happening.

The launches had veered to the right, but Hunter and I
rowed straight in, in the direction of the bunker on the
chart. The whistling stopped abruptly and I could see the
boat guards' heads bobbing as they debated what to do. If
they had run to tell Silver, everything might have turned
out a lot differently; but apparently they had orders to stay
put. They settled down and soon "The Monkeys" was
drifting across the water again.

There was a slight bend in the coast, and I nudged the
tiller to steer us around the other side of it, putting us out of
sight of the launch guards before we landed. I hit the beach
running, with a big bandanna hanging down from the back
of my hat, French Foreign Legion style, against the brutal
sun, and my .32 snug in one hand in case I ran into the boys.

In less than a hundred yards, I reached the bunker.

Apparently it had been built by the U.S. Navy to protect
an antisubmarine watch during the war, and they'd done it
right. It looked to me as if a half-dozen men could have held
off an invading army while they radioed for help. Of course
there was no radio now, only a rusty antenna mast blown
down in a hurricane. But the barbed wire outer fence still
stood intact, while around the perimeter the bunker itself
looked as impregnable as a miniature Fort Knox. They had
built it on a knoll around a spring, a fresh cool-water source
which reminded me of the one thing we didn't have in our
fortified cabin on the ship—we had food, booze, cigs, guns,
and ammo, but no water to speak of.

The bunker walls were thick reinforced concrete and the

space between them and the barbed wire had been cleared of trees so that from inside the shelter the defenders could pick off attackers while they were still trying to negotiate the wire. I was wondering whether we'd be safer in here than aboard the *Hispaniola* when I heard the scream of pain and fear.

No field nurse to Patton's tankers was a stranger to violent death—I'd seen it, fought it, tasted it, and nearly bought it myself once, courtesy of a German .88, but at that scream my heart stopped. "Jim Hawkins is dead," was my first thought.

It's one thing to have been in the war, but a lot more to have been a doctor. There's no time in our work for grief, less for indecision. I made up my mind instantly, ran back to shore, and jumped into the rowboat.

Thank God, Hunter was an old bayman who could row like the devil. We practically flew across the harbor and soon were back aboard the ship.

I found everybody pretty shaken up. My senator was white as a sheet, thinking of the jam he'd gotten us into. And one of the wiseguys looked almost as upset. Smollett nodded toward him and said quietly to me, "That one's not quite the man for the job. He almost fainted, Doc, when he heard the scream. One nudge would probably get him back onto our side."

I told Smollett my plan, and between us we worked out the details.

We put old Redruth, the retired cop, in the belowdecks corridor between the main cabin and the fo'c'sle, heavily armed. Hunter brought the rowboat around under the stern, on the offshore side, so neither the men on the beach nor those sitting on the foredeck could see. Joyce and I started loading her with guns and ammunition, canned food, Silver's fresh-baked bread and pies, and my invaluable black bag and medicine chest.

Meanwhile, the senator and the captain stayed on deck. Smollett braced Israel Hands, who was the senior crewman aboard.

"Mr. Hands," he called. "I have here in *my* hand a forty-five automatic. The weapon Senator Trelawney is pointing your way is a twelve-gauge pump shotgun. Any one of you sons of bitches tries to signal shore, he can kiss his ass good-bye."

They were appropriately stunned, and after some desperate whispering, all six dove down the forehatch, thinking to take us from behind. But when they saw Redruth waiting in the gallery with a pair of double-barrel shotguns, and a belt full of revolvers, they ran forward again, and a head popped out of the hatch.

"Move it or lose it," boomed Captain Smollett.

The head popped down out of sight again and we heard nothing more, for a while at least, from six deeply frightened seamen.

By then, madly heaving whatever gear we could get our hands on, we had the rowboat loaded as heavily as we dared. Hunter, Joyce, and I climbed in, and we headed for shore as fast as they could row.

This second trip really caught the attention of the launch guards. "The Monkeys" stopped in their tracks. And just before we slipped from view behind the little point, one of them jumped ashore and disappeared into the jungle. I had half a mind to steer that way to blow some holes in their launches, but for all I knew Long John Silver was near, and we'd end up rowing into a trap.

Seconds later we hit the beach where we had before, and scrambled to shift the gear to the bunker. All three of us made the first run, heavily laden, and threw the stuff over the barbed wire. We left Joyce to guard it, with sidearms and shotguns, while Hunter and I ran back for more. Back and forth in the thick heat, back and forth again, never stopping for breath, until every last tin can was inside the wire. Then, leaving them to move everything into the bunker, I ran back to the boat and rowed at top speed back to the *Hispaniola*.

We risked a second boatload, which sounds crazier than it was. Silver's men outnumbered us, of course, but we were much better armed. None of those ashore had rifles or shotguns—or so we thought—and even if they'd managed to hide a couple of handguns, we figured that we'd wipe out half a dozen before they could get within pistol range.

The senator was waiting for me on the stern deck, happily recovered from his bout of self-recrimination. He caught my line, tied the boat, and together we loaded as fast as we could. Food and ammo was the cargo again, and the rest of the guns. The handgrenades were tossed overboard in thirty feet of water, which was so clear that we could see metal catching the sunlight on the clean, sandy bottom.

By now the tide was beginning to ebb. The *Hispaniola* was swinging around on her anchor. We could hear voices calling in the direction of the two launches—good news for Joyce and Hunter in the bunker to the east—but a sharp warning to us that it was time to shove off.

"Redruth!"

The old cop retreated from the gallery, as we covered him, and climbed down into the rowboat, which we eased forward along the hull to pick up Captain Smollett.

"Okay, boys," he called. "You hear me?"

Not a peep from the fo'c'sle.

"Abraham Gray—I'm talking to you, Abe Gray."

Still no answer.

"Gray," Captain Smollett resumed, a little louder, "I'm leaving this ship and I'm issuing you a direct order to follow your captain. I know you're a good man way down deep, and the rest of you probably aren't as bad as you think you are. You got thirty seconds to come with me and save your life."

Nothing happened.

"Last chance, Abraham. Make up your mind. I'm risking our necks every second I wait."

From below decks came the sound of a sudden scuffle, the thump of punches. Then out the hatch exploded Abraham Gray with a knife cut streaming blood from his cheek. He ran to the captain like a lost child.

"Here, sir."

He and the captain dropped aboard the deeply laden rowboat and we shoved off, clear of the ship, but a long way from the bunker.

17

Narrative Continued by the Doctor;
The Rowboat's Last Trip

THIS LAST TRIP was a lot different from the others. To begin with, we were way overloaded. Five adults, and three of them—Trelawney, Redruth, and Captain Smollett—men over six feet, were more than the little boat was designed to carry. Add to our weight food, ammunition, and weapons. The transom barely cleared the surface of the harbor and several times we actually shipped water. By the time we'd gone a hundred yards my slacks were soaked. Captain Smollett moved us around to trim the boat, which evened her up a little. Nonetheless, we were afraid to even breathe.

Also, the ebb tide was really starting to flow—a strong choppy current that ran west out of the harbor and then south to the sea through the narrow inlet we'd entered in the morning. Even its little ripples were dangerous to our overloaded boat, but the worst problem was that the current was driving us away from the place we had to land around the point. If we didn't do something fast, it would land us right beside Silver's launches.

"Captain, I can't hold her." I was steering, while he and Redruth worked the oars. "The current's pushing her down. Can you row harder?"

"Not without swamping the boat. Head up, Doc—Sit

down, Senator, she can handle it. Head up, Doc, until you see you're gaining."

I tried to head up, into the current, and it worked after a fashion, but at the cost of slowing our forward motion. "We'll be all day at this rate."

"No choice," said Captain Smollett, pulling harder at his oars. "Gotta keep upstream, otherwise we'll land right in the middle of the launches. If we keep heading into the current, at some point it'll slacken and we can cut into the shore."

"It's easing up already, sir," called Abe Gray in the bow. "I think you can bear off a little, Dr. Livesey."

"Thanks, Abe," I said, treating our former enemy as if nothing had happened. Gray was, we had all agreed, one of us again.

Suddenly the captain spoke, his previously calm voice pitched with anxiety.

"The cannon."

"No sweat," I said, thinking he meant they'd fire on the bunker. "It's too big to get it ashore and even if they did, they'll never drag it through the woods."

"Look behind you, Doctor."

Rowing, he was already facing back. I turned around and saw, to my horror, that they were swarming over the deck cannon, pulling off the tarp that covered my senator's little toy. I think I would have pushed him overboard if I weren't so busy trying to steer, because stashed in the cabin were its high-explosive shells. All they had to do was break down the door and even as I watched one of them headed astern with a fire ax.

"Oh, Jesus," moaned Abraham Gray, sounding like he wished he hadn't changed sides. "Israel was Captain Flint's gunner."

We headed straight for the landing place; fortunately, we had pulled out of the strong tidal current, so I managed to hold the course, despite our necessary slow speed. Unfortunately, however, turning into the shore presented us broadside to the *Hispaniola*'s cannon.

Across the steamy water came the sound of the ax crashing through the cabin door, while that low-down boozer Israel Hands opened the breech to load the first shell.

"Who's the best shot?" asked the captain.

"Senator Trelawney," I said.

"Senator, you wanta knock off one of them bastards? Hands, if you can," said the captain.

Trelawney, my sometimes silly senator, was cool as steel. He picked up a rifle, jacked a slug into the chamber, and peered down the barrel. There was something frighteningly reptilian in the steadiness of his eye, and I remember thinking that there were things from our youth that would never leave us.

"Now," said Captain Smollett. "Easy with the gun, Senator, or you'll swamp us. Okay, stand by to trim her when he aims. All yours, Senator."

He stopped rowing and Senator Trelawney swung the barrel gently toward the *Hispaniola*. We all leaned the other way to counterbalance, and it was done so neatly that we didn't ship a drop.

They, by this time, were swinging the cannon our way. Hands, standing right behind it, lining it up, was most exposed. But just as Trelawney fired, Hands stooped down to adjust something. The bullet passed right through the space where his head had been and dropped one of the others to the deck.

He howled, a cry echoed by his companions, who threw themselves down, and by the rest of Silver's gangsters, who suddenly burst out of the trees and piled into the launches.

"Here come the boats," I cried. A second later an engine roared to life.

"We're heading in," cried the captain, rowing like mad. "Doesn't matter if we swamp her now. If we don't get to shore we've had it."

"They're only taking one of the launches," I said. "I think the rest are coming around by shore to cut us off."

"It's a long way around," said Smollett, rowing harder. "They're not our problem. It's that damned deck gun. My own mother couldn't miss at this range. Senator, yell as soon as Hands zeroes in on us. I'll back water. Rest of you pray."

We were moving pretty fast by then for a boat so overloaded, but which luckily hadn't shipped much water. We were close in, too, maybe another forty of Smollett's strokes and we would hit a narrow strip of beach that the ebbing tide had exposed. We were also luckily around the little point, shielding us from the launch, whose engine we could hear firing balkily as they tried to back her out of the shallows. The tide, which had delayed us, had grounded them. But, as Smollett said, the real danger was the cannon.

"I'd love to stop and knock off another man," said the captain.

It was doubtful that even the senator's shooting could help at this point. Israel Hands's crew had barely looked at their wounded pal. He wasn't dead, and I could see him trying to crawl away. His friends, however, were concentrating on the cannon.

"I'll make it Mr. Hands this time," said the senator, raising his weapon again with the same unblinking gaze.

"Hold it!" echoed the captain.

He backed water with a mighty heave that drove the stern right under. The cannon roared in the same instant. The high-explosive shell thundered overhead like an express train. Where it landed, we never knew because it failed to explode on impact—another of Mr. Blandly's surplus bargains, for which I am eternally in his debt. It came close enough to part our hair, however, and either the noise or its wind contributed to our disaster.

The boat sank stern first, quite gently, in three feet of water, leaving Captain Smollett and me facing each other standing submerged to our waists. The other three fell head over heels and came up drenched and spitting water.

So far so good. Nobody was hurt or killed and we could wade ashore. But everything we'd been carrying was in the bottom of the boat. Much worse, few of our guns were usable. I had snatched my shotgun off my knees and my .32 from my waistband and held them over my head. As for Captain Smollett, he had slung a rifle over his shoulder by the sling, and like the rough and ready man he had turned out to be, had kept it high and dry with the butt in the air. The others had gone down with the boat.

If that weren't bad enough, we heard voices getting close in the woods along the shore. We were in danger of being cut off from the bunker. If they attacked the bunker instead, Hunter and Joyce might not be able to hold them off. Hunter was solid, we knew that. But Joyce was an easygoing little guy, more the sort to hold your coat than stand shoulder to shoulder in the trenches.

Without a second to lose, we waded ashore, leaving behind the rowboat and damn near half our food and ammunition.

18

Narrative Continued by the Doctor;
End of the First Day's Fighting

WE RAN LIKE hell through the woods between us
and the bunker. But at every step we could hear Silver's men catching up, first their voices, soon their pounding boots, and the crackling of branches as they crashed through the underbrush.

I saw we had a fight on our hands, and snicked off the safety on my shotgun.

"Captain," I said to Smollett, "the Senator's the best shot. Give him your rifle."

Smollett handed it over and Trelawney, silent and cool as he'd been since we fled the ship, checked it out with sure hands. Abe Gray was unarmed, so I tossed him my .32 and it was a good feeling all around to see him check the loads and spin the cylinder like a man looking forward to a firefight. It was pretty clear that our recent convert was a real find.

Thirty yards ahead we came to the edge of the woods and saw the bunker. We reached the barbed wire in the middle of the south side just as seven of them—led by Job Anderson, the bosun—arrived yelling at the top of their lungs at the southwest corner.

For a split second they hesitated, as if startled to see us; and before they recovered, not only the senator and I, but also Joyce and Hunter from the bunker, had time to open fire. It was a pretty ragged volley, for we were sort of startled too, to find ourselves face to face, but it won the moment. One of them actually fell, while his pals ran for it.

Reloading, we walked the wire perimeter to find the one who had fallen. Shot through the heart and stone dead.

We started to congratulate ourselves on a close call well handled when a pistol cracked in the brush, a slug whistled by my ear, and poor Tom Redruth staggered and fell on his face. Both the senator and I returned the fire, but with nothing to see but jungle, we were wasting bullets. Reloading again, we had a look at Tom. The captain and Gray were already bent over him and I saw immediately that he didn't have a chance.

I think our shooting at the jungle had the effect of scattering Silver's gang. Whatever, they didn't bother us as we hoisted Tom over the wire and carried him groaning and bleeding into the bunker.

The poor old guy had neither complained nor questioned any of our orders since the fight began. He had held them off like the Lone Ranger in the gallery. He was twenty years older than any of us. And now, stodgy old grump that he was, he was our first to die.

The senator knelt beside him, crying like a baby.

"Is my number up, Doc?" Tom asked.

My "doctor shield" melted in my hands. I knelt too, and kissed his forehead and told him he was God's child now.

"Son of a bitch. Wish I nailed a few of the bastards first."

"Tom," wept the senator, "will you forgive me?"

"What the hell for? It weren't your fault—but if it makes you happy, sure."

After a few moments of staring silently at the reinforced concrete ceiling, Tom said he thought a prayer might not be a bad idea. Then, without another word, he was gone.

In the meantime, the captain had been emptying the biggest, most marvelously stuffed pockets I had ever seen on a man. He was a walking PX, full of all the stuff the rest of us hadn't thought to bring—an American flag, a Bible, a coil of strong rope, a pen and the log book, and, bless him, a carton of cigarettes. I felt an almost carnal sense of gratitude. While Tom was dying, the captain had gone out and cut down a fair-sized pine tree with a bowie knife, stripped off its branches, and with Hunter's help erected it at the corner of the bunker. Climbing onto the roof, he attached the flag.

It seemed to make him feel better. He hurried back inside and got busy counting up our supplies. He worked singlemindedly, and even came up with another flag to cover the body.

"Get ahold of yourself," he said, clapping the senator's shoulder. "He's fine now—shot in the line of duty—they'll have a color guard lined up at the Pearly Gates. They don't tell you that in Sunday school, but it's a fact."

Then he motioned me aside.

"How many weeks before they start missing you, Doc?"

"Months," I said. "Not weeks. Blandly'll come looking eventually, if he thinks there's cash in it, otherwise . . . You figure it out."

Smollett scratched his head. "I was afraid of that . . . Well, unless someone pulls a heretofore invisible rabbit out of their hat, we got problems."

"Which problems, exactly?" I asked.

"It's a damn shame we lost the second load is what I mean. We're pretty well armed, thank the Lord, but rations are short. Real short. In fact so short, Doc, that just between you and me, we're probably better off without that extra mouth." He nodded toward Tom's body under the flag.

Just then, with another express-train roar and whistle, a shell passed over the roof and exploded far off in the woods.

"Oh yeah?" said the captain. "Blast away, you sons of bitches, you'll blow that gun right off the foredeck and your heads with it."

Their aim got better. Their second try crumped down in

the sand between the bunker and barbed wire, scattering sand.

"Captain," said the senator, "they can't see the bunker from the ship. They must be aiming at the flag. Maybe we ought to—"

"Strike colors? Never!" cried the captain. Brave, of course, silly, perhaps, but at that moment it gave us all courage. And it was a clear message to Silver's gang that we weren't afraid of them or their cannon.

All evening they thundered at us. Shell after shell flew over or fell short into the trees or buried itself harmlessly in the soft sand. Several exploded on the roof; the sound was deafening, but, as Captain Smollett, who had little good to say about the regular navy, said, "Those Seabees knew their business when they built this place." In fact, other than ear-ringing noise, the *Hispaniola*'s deck gun did very little damage to either the inhabitants of the bunker or their morale.

"There's one good thing," said the captain. "The bastards probably aren't hanging around the woods for this and the tide's been ebbing quite a while, so our supplies should be above water. Volunteers to go get the rations!"

Gray and Hunter leapt front and center. Heavily armed, they snuck out of the wire, but it was a bust. The "bastards" were braver than we thought, or, more likely, put greater faith in Israel Hands's gunnery. Gray and Hunter reported that they were carrying off our supplies themselves and wading them out to one of the launches, which lay close in, her prop ticking over to hold her against the current. Long John Silver was at the tiller, in command. And every man had a rifle from some secret magazine they must have hid on the ship or found on the island.

Captain Smollett sat down on an ammunition box, opened his log book on his knees, and started writing. I read over his shoulder:

Alexander Smollett, master;
Janet Livesey, ship's doctor;
Abraham Gray, carpenter's
mate; John Trelawney, owner;
John Hunter, owner's employee,
bayman, and Richard Joyce,
owner's employee, landsman —
the last loyal men of the
ship's company — with supplies
for ten days at short rations,
come ashore this day and flew
the Stars and Stripes over
the bunker on Treasure Island.
Thomas Redruth, owner's
employee, landsman, shot
resisting mutiny; James
Hawkins, cabin boy ...

And at the same time I was wondering what had happened
to poor Jim, a shout came from the land side.

"Somebody's calling us," said Hunter, who was standing guard.

"Doctor! Senator! Captain! Hey, Hunter, is that you?" came the cries.

And I ran to the door in time to see Jim Hawkins, safe and sound, come slithering through the wire.

19

Story Resumed by Jim Hawkins;
The Holdouts in the Bunker

W H E N Ben Gun saw the American flag he grabbed my arm.

"Looks like your pals in there."

"More likely Silver," I said, peering through the wire with little hope of seeing a friendly face.

"He'd never fly the Stars and Stripes, kid. You can bet your bottom dollar that's your pals. Looks like there's been a bit of a donnybrook and your people came out on top. Abandoned ship and dug into that old sub patrol bunker that Flint restored. See that wire, all new strung? Flint had the brains, all right. He was one piece of work; only thing he couldn't beat was the booze. Feared no one, except, of course, Silver—Silver being such a gentle soul."

"Maybe so . . . I guess we better join them."

"No, Jim, not me. You're a good kid, I'm sure, but you're only a boy. Now, Ben Gunn is a smart guy. A tall rum and Coke wouldn't get me in there, where you're going—not till I see your senator and get his promise. And you won't forget what I told you, remember: 'Gunn had plenty to keep him busy,' you'll tell him. 'Plenty to look for.' Get it?" He gave me another big wink. " 'And plenty of time to look for it.'

"And when your senator says 'Bring me Ben Gunn,' you'll know where to find him, won't you, Jim? Right where you found him today. And the one he sends looking for me?

Carries a white flag. And he comes alone. Right? Oh, and also, you'll say, 'Ben Gunn, he's got his reasons.' "

"Okay," I said. "I think I get it. You want to make a proposition to the senator. And you want to see him, or the doctor. And you'll be where I found you. Anything else?"

" 'And when?' you ask. Anytime between noon and three."

"Okay. Can I go now?"

"You'll remember?" he asked anxiously. " 'Plenty of time to look. And reasons of his own,' you'll say. That's the main thing. Man to man. Okay, then"—still holding me— "run along. Only, Jim, if you see Silver, you wouldn't rat on Ben Gunn, would you? Wild horses couldn't drag it out of you. 'Absolutely not,' you say. And if those sons of bitches sleep on the beach tonight, want to bet there'll be some widows in the morning?"

Suddenly he was interrupted by a loud bang, and a cannon shell screamed through the trees and blew up less than a hundred yards from where we were standing. We ran in opposite directions.

For a good hour boom after boom shook the island and shells kept exploding through the woods. I jumped and dodged from cover to cover, chased by explosions that sent splinters and shrapnel whistling around my head. But near the end of the attack, I began to get my courage back, though I didn't go anywhere near the bunker, where most of the shells landed. Instead, I circled in a long, head-ducking, belly-crawling detour to the east, and crept down among the trees along the shore.

The sun had just gone down, and the sea breeze was blowing the trees and ruffling the gray surface of the harbor. The tide was out, and broad sand flats lay above water. The air was cold. The chilly wind cut through my jacket.

The *Hispaniola* was still there, tugging at her anchor. I saw a flash from her deck gun and another shell shrieked overhead on its way to the bunker. It turned out to be the last, for the cannon had broken loose under the strain—as Captain Smollett had predicted back in New York—and leaned drunkenly, its muzzle touching the deck. The men firing yelled at one another for a while, and then there was silence, and the bird flocks began settling down on the water.

I hid for a while, watching a gang of men attack something with axes on the beach near the bunker—the poor rowboat, I learned later. Off near the river mouth a huge fire glowed among the trees. The launches started shuttling back and forth between the beach fire and the ship. The men, who'd been so grumpy earlier, were singing happily—with that especially loud off-key note I remembered from late-night drinkers in my father's bar.

I figured I could risk a run to the bunker.

I was pretty far down the low beach that rimmed the east end of the harbor and connected at low tide to Skeleton Island. As I stood up I saw farther down a tall, white rock rising out of the sand by some bushes. Ben Gunn's rock, I thought, where he had hidden his boat.

Then I circled through the woods, all the way behind the bunker on the shore side, and was welcomed back by my friends.

I told my story, heard theirs, and had a look around.

The bunker was made of tree trunks and concrete, buried half underground, except for a sort of porch-entrance enclosing the freshwater spring, which bubbled into a fifty-gallon steel drum with its top and bottom cut out and sunk into the sand. The only other "comfort" was a crude wood stove made out of another steel drum.

All the trees on the hill and inside the barbed wire had been cut down to build the thick walls, leaving only stumps to show what a nice little forest the slope had been before the Seabees had come. The soil around them was eroded and washed away or buried by sand drifts. The only green in the cut area—ferns and little bushes—grew around a little stream fed by the spring, which trickled down the slope into the woods. Trees loomed close to the wire—too close for defense, said Captain Smollett. The woods were tall and dense, fir on the land side, with some live oaks mixed in to seaward.

The cold evening sea breeze that I had felt on the beach whistled through every crack, turning the bunker into an icebox. A gritty icebox, as the wind blew fine, dusty sand into everything. We had sand in our eyes, sand in our teeth, sand in our supper, sand in the spring, where it danced in the current like those snow scenes on the teacher's desk. The stove's chimney had rusted out, so the only way for the smoke to get out was to drift out a hole in the roof, which it did eventually, after circling the room like a forest fog. Everybody was coughing and wiping their eyes.

Add to the sand and smoke and the memory of the recent artillery attack the fact that Gray, the new man, looked like Frankenstein's monster, with a bloody bandage covering his face where the mutineers had cut him, and the sight of poor old Tom Redruth, lying stiff as a board under Old Glory.

If we'd been allowed to just sit there, we'd have gotten depressed. But not under Captain Smollett's command.

"Now hear this!"

He assigned watches. Dr. Livesey, Gray, and I were one watch; the senator, Hunter, and Joyce, the other. Tired or not, two were sent out for firewood; two more were ordered to check the perimeter wire. Dr. Livesey was made cook. I was told to stand guard at the door, while Captain Smollett himself made the rounds visiting each of us and lending a hand with anything we needed.

Every now and then Dr. Livesey would retreat to the door for some fresh air and to rest her eyes, which were red and swollen from the smoke. Whenever she did, she'd talk to me.

"Smollett is a hell of an officer," she confided once. "We're lucky to have him."

Another time she came out and was silent for a while. Then she cocked her head and looked at me.

"What do you think of Ben Gunn, Jim?"

"I'm not sure. I think he might be nuts."

"Maybe," said the doctor. "But a man who's been chewing his nails for three years on a desert island is bound to act a little strange. People get odd when they're alone too much . . . What does he want, Fig Newtons?"

"I told him we had plenty on the ship."

"He's welcome to them, provided we get our ship back."

"I told him that. I figured the captain wouldn't mind sharing."

"What did he say?"

"He started ranting about being rich."

Captain Smollett said we had to bury Tom. While the bunker was cool, it was sure to get hot under the noonday sun, and who knew how long we'd be trapped with the body. So before eating supper, we dug a grave in the sand, and stood around for a while with our hats off.

Quite a lot of firewood had been dragged inside, but not enough for Captain Smollett. "More wood," he ordered, shaking his head at the pile. "First thing in the morning." Then, when we'd finished the Dinty Moore beef stew Dr. Livesey had heated up, the senator, Captain Smollett, and Dr. Livesey huddled to figure out what to do next.

It looked to me like they had no idea. Supplies were too low. Silver's men could starve us out, long before any help arrived. Our best bet, they decided, was to keep on killing mutineers until they either surrendered or ran away on the *Hispaniola*. They were already down to fifteen men from their original nineteen. Two more were wounded, one of them—the man Senator Trelawney had shot beside the cannon—critically wounded, if not already dead. So every time we got a chance to take a shot at them, we should take it, without risking our lives too much. We couldn't afford to lose anybody. And besides that, we had two things going for us—booze and the fetid tropical climate.

The booze was flowing already. We could hear them, half a mile off, roaring and singing the night away. As for our friend the climate, Dr. Livesey bet "dollars to doughnuts" that camped by the marsh without medicine, half of them would be flat on their backs in less than a week.

"So," she said, "if we're not all shot dead first, they'll be happy to just sail away and go bother somebody else."

"First ship I ever lost," growled Captain Smollett.

I was very tired, needless to say. And when I finally fell asleep, after tossing and turning reliving the long day, I slept like a log.

The others had been up for hours, had already eaten breakfast and carried in a huge mess of firewood, when I was awakened by a loud commotion and excited voices.

"White flag!" I heard someone say. "Truce. They want to talk!" Then, right after that, an astonished shout: "It's Silver!"

I jumped up, rubbed the sleep from my eyes, and ran to look.

20

Silver the Diplomat

THERE THEY WERE, two men just inside the wire, one waving a dirty white dishrag tied to a stick, the other, Long John Silver himself, waiting calmly for our reaction.

It was still quite early in the morning, and bone-chilling cold. The sky was clear and the treetops were lit by the sun. But down where Silver and his flagbearer waited was deep in shadow, and they stood to their knees in an eerie white mist that had oozed from the swamp in the night. The cold and the fog proved once again Dr. Livesey's opinion that the island was not a healthy place.

"Everybody stay inside," said the captain. "Ten to one it's a trick."

Then he called, "Who goes? Halt or we shoot!"

"Truce flag!" cried Silver.

The captain stayed well inside the entry porch. He called over his shoulder to us, "Dr. Livesey's watch on lookout. Doc, take the north side; Jim, the east; Gray, west. Everybody else load guns. Heads up! Move!"

Then he addressed Silver. "What do you want?"

The flag-waver answered. "Captain Silver, sir, coming aboard to make a deal."

"Captain Silver? Never heard of him. Who's he?" asked the captain, adding to himself, "Captain my ass."

Long John Silver answered, "Me, sir. These poor guys elected me captain, after you deserted, sir"—leaning heavily on the word *deserted*. All I ask is your promise, Captain Smollett, of safe passage into your fort and one minute to get out of range before you shoot."

"I don't want to talk to you," said Captain Smollett. "You want to talk to me? Come on in. Any monkey business, we'll blow your heads off."

"Fair enough, Captain," Long John answered cheerfully. "You're an officer and a gentleman."

The man holding the flag tried to hold Silver back, which wasn't surprising, considering the captain's blunt reply. But Silver laughed at him like it was all a big joke, and slapped him on the back. Then he waded through the fog up to the wire, tossed his crutch over it, grabbed one of the posts, and with the strength and agility of an acrobat, flung himself over the high fence and onto the cleared ground inside.

I have to admit I was so interested in what was happening that I wasn't paying attention to my sentry duties. In fact, I had wandered away from the eastern loophole to stand behind the captain, who had sat on the porch steps with his elbows on his knees and a shotgun in his hands. He was whistling to himself, "She'll Be Comin' 'Round the Mountain."

Silver had an awful time climbing up our hill. The soft sand, the steep slope, and the tree stumps made him almost helpless on his crutch. But he stuck to it and finally reached the captain and threw him a snappy salute. He was all gussied up in a huge blue naval greatcoat with gleaming brass buttons, and an officer's cap with gold "scrambled eggs" on its shiny visor.

"Here you are," said the captain. "Have a seat."

"You ain't gonna invite me indoors, Captain? Hell of a cold morning to sit outside in the sand."

"Look, Silver," said the captain. "If you'd stayed honest, you'd be sitting in your nice warm galley right now. You brought this on yourself. You're either my ship's cook—where you were treated like gold—or you're low-down thieving mutinying scum, in which case there's a hot seat reserved for you at Sing Sing."

"Okay, Captain," said the cook, sitting down on the sand. "You'll just have to help me stand up, is all. Nice little place you got here. Hey, there's Jim. Top of the morning, Jim. Hello, Dr. Livesey, how you doing? Cigs holding up? Well, here you all are, one big happy family, so to speak."

"If you have anything to say, mister, spit it out," said the captain.

"Right you are, Captain Smollett. Business first. Straight talk. Okay. I'll admit up front that was one cute maneuver you pulled last night. Very slick. Some of you are pretty good commandos. I'll also admit some of my boys are kind of shook up over it—maybe all shook up; hell, maybe I was shook up too; maybe that's why I'm here to talk turkey. But get this and get it straight, Captain, it won't work a second time. You can bet the farm on that. We'll post sentries. We'll ease off a bit on the booze. Maybe you think we were all drunk as skunks last night. But you better believe I was sober. I was only dead-tired sleeping. If I'd woken up a second earlier, I'd have caught you red-handed. And by the way, he wasn't dead when I got to him. He just looked that way."

"So?" says Captain Smollett, cool as a cucumber.

He hadn't a clue what Silver was talking about, but he never showed it. But I began to realize what had happened last night. I remembered Ben Gunn's last words. And I realized he must have paid the boys a visit after they passed out drunk around their fire. I had a funny feeling we now had only fourteen enemies left to fight.

"Here's the deal," said Silver. "We came for Flint's gold and we're going to leave with Flint's gold. That's a given. No debate. But you would like to save your lives, I suppose. That's your given. You have a chart, right?"

"Get stuffed, Silver."

"I know you have it. No point in getting all snippy. No way to act. What I mean is, we want your chart. Remember, I never meant any harm."

"I suppose that little workout with the deck gun was all in fun," interrupted the captain. "We know exactly what you meant to do. Your problem is you can't do it, so suddenly you want to talk."

The captain pulled out a pack of Luckies and lit up.

"If Abe Gray—"

"Hold it!" cried Smollett. "Gray said nothing and I didn't ask. I'd see you and him and this whole island blown clear out of the water first. In case you were wondering."

This little temper tantrum cooled Silver down. He pulled himself together and went on calmly.

"Fine by me. And seeing as how you're going to enjoy a smoke I think I'll join you."

And he lighted a Camel. They sat silently smoking for a while, sometimes looking each other in the face, then glancing away to blow smoke, then leaning forward to spit. Watching them was like going to a movie.

"Okay," said Silver after a while. "Here's the deal. You give us the chart to find the gold, and stop shooting innocent sailors, and stop bashing their heads in at night when they sleep. You do that, you get a choice: you can come aboard the ship, after we find the gold, and I give you my word we'll drop you off someplace safe ashore. Or, if you're afraid some of the boys might be too rough on you, you can stay right here and I give you my word I'll report your position to the first ship I see and send them to pick you up. Now is that a deal? Fair as fair can be. And a lot better than anyone else would give people in your position. And I hope," he said, raising his voice, "that everyone else hiding in the fort realizes this generous offer is open to all of youse."

Captain Smollett stood up and ground his cigarette under his heel.

"Is that it?"

"In total," said Silver. "Turn it down and all you'll get from me is hot lead and cold steel."

"Okay," said the captain. "Now hear this: if you'll march in here, one by one, unarmed, I'll slap the cuffs on you and take you home to a fair trial in New York. If you won't, my name is Alexander Smollett, I'm flying the American flag, and I'll send you all to Davy Jones. You can't find the gold. You don't have a man among you smart enough to navigate the ship. You can't fight us—Gray, there, broke loose from five of you. You're dead in the water, Mr. Silver, your engine's shot, your main bearing's burned up. I'm here to tell you what you already know: it's all over but the tears. And that's the last kind word you'll hear from me. Next time we meet I'll blow your head off. Weigh anchor, mister. Haul your ass out of here. Double time!"

It would take a thousand words to describe Silver's face. His eyes bulged with rage. He ground his cigarette into the sand.

"Give me a hand up!"

"Not me," said the captain.

"Who'll help me stand?" he roared.

None of us moved. Growling, cursing, he crawled over the sand until he got ahold of the porch and pulled himself onto his crutch. Then he spat in the spring.

"That's what I think of you. Before an hour's up, I'll blow the roof off your bunker. Laugh? Go ahead, laugh. You'll be laughing out of the other side of your mouth. Those that die'll be the lucky ones."

He cursed us all to hell, plowed down the sand, and was helped over the wire—after four or five tries—by the man with the white dishrag. A second later, he vanished in the trees.

21

The Attack

THE CAPTAIN WATCHED Silver until he vanished, then turned to us inside the bunker. His face went purple. None of us were at our posts, except Gray. It was the first time we had ever seen Captain Smollett really angry, a memorable sight.

"Battle stations!" he roared. "What the blazes are you all gawking at?" And then, as we slunk swiftly back to our stations, he said, "Gray. I'm noting in the log that you stood by your duty like a seaman. Senator Trelawney, I'm shocked at your behavior. Shocked! And as for you, Dr. Livesey, if you'd served General Patton like that, we'd be speaking German."

We on the doctor's watch were all back staring out our loopholes, and the rest were busy loading spare weapons, and if anyone wasn't blushing with embarrassment, I didn't see him.

The captain glowered a while in silence. Then he spoke.

"Now hear this. I let Silver have it with both barrels on purpose. We'll be boarded in an hour, just like he promised. We're outnumbered, obviously, better than two to one. On the other hand, we're inside, under cover. And up until a minute ago, I'd have said we had the added advantage of discipline. So, if you give your all, I have no doubt we can beat 'em."

Pep talk concluded, he made the rounds and saw, as he said, that the coast was clear.

On either short end of the bunker, east and west, were two loopholes or shooting slits—horizontal openings about big enough to pass a bowling ball through. There were two more slits on the south side where the porch was. In back on the north side, five openings.

We had twenty guns for the seven of us, rifles, shotguns, and side arms. We had stacked the firewood into four separate piles and used them as tables to hold the extra guns and ammunition. On a pile in the middle we had heaped a bunch of bayonets and machetes, originally purchased to hack through the jungle.

"Douse the fire," said the captain. "It's warmed up and we don't need the smoke in our eyes."

A bucket from the spring put an end to the fire.

"Hawkins hasn't eaten breakfast. Jim, grab a handful and eat it at your post. Move, boy. You'll want a full belly when the fighting starts. Hunter, give everybody a shot of rye."

While this was going on, the captain put the final touches on his defense plan.

"Doc, you'll take the door. Fire through the porch. Make sure you stay under cover. Hunter, take the east side. Joyce, the west. Senator, you're the best shot, you and Gray cover the north side. You've got five big slits there. There's our weakest side. If they get up to the wall they can pick us off in here like rats. Hawkins, you and me, we're not such hot shots. We'll be standing by to reload and lend a hand. Stick close."

The chill was definitely gone. The tropical sun rocketed into the sky, burning away the mist, and when it cleared the treetops that shaded our bunker, we began to bake like apple pies. Sweat poured down our faces and sap oozed from the logs that supported the roofs. Coats and jackets went flying. Pretty soon, stripped down to T-shirts and shorts, we looked like a gym class standing at our posts.

A long hour passed slowly, until we were sweating as much from nerves as from the heat. "This is dull as church," said Captain Smollett.

But just then things turned lively.

"Captain?" called polite little Joyce in his quiet voice. "Sir, am I supposed to shoot if I see anybody?"

"Shoot! Damned right, shoot!"

"Thank you, sir."

We heard nothing. Smollett bounded across the bunker. "Do you see them?"

"Not yet, sir."

The exchange set us all on edge, straining ears and eyes. The gunners steadied their weapons in the slits. The captain paced the middle of the bunker, his mouth a hard line, frowns creasing his face.

A few more seconds ticked by. Suddenly Joyce whipped up his gun and fired a single shot that boomed loudly in the confined space. An instant later, a scattered volley answered from the woods. Bullets pocked and whined on the outside walls, but none came in. And just as suddenly, things were quiet again. We saw not a leaf move, nor the gleam of a face, nor the glint of sun on a gun barrel.

"Did you hit him, Joyce?" asked the captain.

"I don't think so."

"Doc? How many did you see on your side?"

"Three shooting. Two close together. One farther west."

"Three," repeated the captain. "How many on yours, Senator?"

"Hard to tell, Captain. I counted seven. Gray thinks eight or nine."

"They'll hit us from the north," said Captain Smollett. And it did seem as if the shots from the other sides had been for show. Still, he left the defenses as they were, pointing out that anyone who got through the fence and alongside the bunker could pick us off at his leisure through the slits.

That was about all the thinking time we got. With bloodcurdling yells from the north side, seven men charged out of the woods straight at the barbed wire. The rest started shooting from the woods again, and a bullet through the doorway knocked the doctor's gun out of her hands.

The attackers swarmed over the wire, climbing like monkeys. The senator and Gray fired again and again. Three men fell, one tumbling inside the fence, two outside. One, wounded, jumped up and ran back into the trees.

Two down. One running for his life. But four had made it inside the wire, while those hidden in the woods laid down a heavy fire on the bunker.

The four who got inside ran straight at us, shooting, while those in the trees cheered them on. We fired too fast to take aim, and there were no hits. In an instant, they scrambled up the hill and were on us like a pack of wild dogs.

The head of Job Anderson, the bosun, filled the middle shooting slit. "Kill 'em!" he roared. "Kill 'em all!"

Another pirate reached through Hunter's shooting slit, yanked his gun barrel out of his hands, and slammed his head with the stock, dropping poor Hunter on the floor. A third man ran all the way around the bunker without a shot hitting him, and exploded through the door, swinging a machete at Dr. Livesey.

They had turned the tables on us in a second. One moment we were firing from cover at enemies in the open; now *we* were exposed, attacked from every side. Chaos. Muzzles flashed in the gloom. Gunshots, cries, and loud groans filled my ears.

"Out! Get out! Fight 'em in the open!" yelled Captain Smollett. "Machetes."

I grabbed a machete from the pile. Someone seizing another cut me across the knuckles. I hardly felt it. I ran out the door, and there in the clear sunlight Dr. Livesey was struggling with the man with the machete. He had a hairy arm around her throat and was raising the long knife high.

Before I could even try to help her, she twisted one of her revolvers behind her and shot him in the gut.

The rest of them came swarming over the wire to join the fight, led by a big salvage diver with a red watch cap and a bayonet.

"Around the back," cried the captain. "Regroup! Regoup! Around the back!" But through the storm of battle I heard a change in his voice.

I rounded the corner of the bunker, machete raised, and found myself face to face with Job Anderson. The bosun swung his rifle over his shoulder to brain me with it. I had no time to be afraid, much less think of moving. I remember the barrel flashing in the sun. I flinched to one side, stumbled, and rolled down the slope.

The big bosun pounced to swing again. Abe Gray, right behind me, cut him down with his machete. Another attacker had been shot right at the shooting slit, just as he was about to fire into the bunker, and lay dying in agony. The doctor had killed a third with her .32. Of the four who had scaled the wire, the last dropped his machete and scrambled back over, fleeing for his life.

"Stop him!" cried Dr. Livesey, shooting as fast as she could pull the trigger at the man already out of range.

But everyone else was too stunned to fire and he made his getaway, leaving behind four dead men inside the wire and the one who had fallen outside.

"Back inside. Get under cover."

Dr. Livesey, Abraham Gray, and I ran full speed for the bunker, before the survivors could start shooting again from the woods.

Inside, we discovered we'd paid hard for our victory. Hunter lay stunned beneath his shooting slit. Joyce, shot through the head, slumped beside him. In the middle of the room, the senator was holding up the captain, both men white as sheets.

"Captain's hit."

"Did they run?" whispered Captain Smollett.

"All gone," said the doctor, coolly stuffing fresh loads into her revolver. "We got five."

"Five! That evens things up a bit. Only nine of 'em left. Well done, mates."

But adding up *our* dead and wounded, we were down to four still on their feet—the Senator, Abe Gray, Dr. Livesey, and me.

PART FIVE

I GO SAILING

22

How My Sea Adventure Began

T HEY'VE HAD A bellyful," said the captain. We had
our bunker to ourselves, and time to take care of the
wounded and eat some lunch. The senator and I cooked
outside, preferring the danger of getting shot from the trees
to the groans and screams of Dr. Livesey's patients.

The attacker who'd been shot at the shooting slit died as
she tried to remove the bullet. Hunter never regained con-
sciousness. He lingered all day long, lungs rattling like Billy
Bones's after his stroke in my parents' hotel; his chest
had been crushed, his skull fractured. He died late in the
night.

Captain Smollett was badly shot up. Anderson's slug—
the first that hit—had broken his shoulder blade and grazed
his lung; but the second shot was just a flesh wound that
tore up some muscles in his calf. He would recover, Dr.
Livesey promised, but slowly. She warned him not to try to
walk or move his arm, or even speak, which pretty much put
our leader out of commission.

My accidental machete slice was only a nick. Dr. Livesey
stuck some Band-Aids on my knuckles, gave me a tickle in
the ribs, and one of her fierce, fast hugs.

After lunch she and the senator sat and talked with the
captain. When they were done, Dr. Livesey put on her hat
and French Foreign Legion neckcloth, loaded her pockets

with pistols and ammunition, and slipped the chart inside her blouse. Then she picked up a short-barreled shotgun, climbed through the wire on the north side, and sauntered into the trees.

Gray and I were sitting out of the way at the far end of the bunker. When the doctor walked out, the cigarette Gray had been firing up dropped from his open mouth and fell smoldering and unnoticed at his feet. "What in—Is the doc crazy?"

"I always thought she was the sanest one we have."

"I'll tell you, mate, if *she's* sane, then I'm nuts. Where in hell is she going?"

I thought it over. "Bet you a buck she's going to see Ben Gunn."

I won that bet, eventually, but at that moment, sweltering in the bunker as the sun burned hotter and hotter, I began to get my own crazy idea. I envied the doctor walking through cool, shady woods while I roasted in the stink of sweat and sand and poor dead bodies. The more I thought of her in the clean shade the less I could stand the bunker.

Going about my cabin boy chores—cleaning up the bunker, washing the lunch dishes—I got more and more fed up with the place, the sickening smells and the heat. Finally, alone and unnoticed among the food crates, I stuffed my pockets with Mounds Bars.

I'll admit I was an idiot, if not an out-and-out jerk. But at least I was thinking ahead—no matter what happened, the Mounds Bars would keep me from starving.

Then I sort of sidled over to the guns and when no one was looking, stuffed a couple of small ones in my belt.

I had a plan to head down to the beach on the spit that protected the anchorage from the sea and find the white rock that hid Ben Gunn's boat. It seemed like a good idea at the time, but I knew they wouldn't let me out alone. My only chance was to go AWOL when nobody was watching.

Some might say that "absent without leave" or "going

over the hill" are polite terms for deserting your friends, but I thought I had a good reason. And I wanted out of that sweltering bunker so bad I could taste it.

I got a lucky break. The captain started bleeding. The senator and Gray got busy changing the bandages, and the coast was clear. I ran for it, out the door, through the wire, and into the woods before anybody noticed.

This was my second dumb stunt, worse than when I jumped into the shore leave boat, because I was leaving only two unwounded men to guard the bunker. But, like the first, it helped save us all.

I headed straight for the east coast of the island to go down the sea side of the spit so Silver's gang wouldn't see me from the anchorage. It was still warm and sunny, though late in the afternoon. As I weaved through the tall trees toward the distant rumble of the pounding surf, leaves and branches began rustling and waving hard in the sea breeze. Nearer the surf I began to feel a cool wind penetrate the trees, and then a little farther along I found myself on the edge of the woods looking out over the water, which spread blue and sunny to the horizon.

The sea is never quiet around Treasure Island. The air may be dead calm, and the surface smooth in the sunlight, but giant rollers still march in from the east and thunder onto the outer beaches. You can hear them almost everywhere on the island, so steady and monotonous a sound that you often don't notice.

Out on the barrier beach I ran beside the surf, breathing in the cool salt air and noise, reveling in my escape from the hot bunker. I headed south a ways, then crept inland through the brush onto the center ridge, where I could see the anchorage.

The breeze had tapered off and a fog was creeping into the harbor from the south. While the sea behind me was crashing on the sand, the sheltered water was still as a mirror. So still did the *Hispaniola* ride at anchor that she was reflected absolutely perfectly upside down, as if she were floating hull to hull beside a second ship identical in every detail, right down to her useless radio mast.

A launch lay alongside, Silver at the outboard—I would have recognized him at twice the distance. Two guys were leaning over the stern, one with a red cap—the big salvage diver who'd led the second attack over the wire. They seemed to be joking around, though at that distance, over a mile, I couldn't hear what they were saying. A horrible scream scared me half to death before I realized it was only Captain Flint, whose bright feathers I could just make out, adorning Silver's shoulder.

They shoved off and headed for shore. The man with the red cap, whom they'd left aboard the *Hispaniola*, headed below.

With the sun gone down behind Spyglass Hill and the fog coming in heavily, it began to get very dark. I had to step on it if I was going to find Ben Gunn's boat.

The white rock was still about an eighth of a mile down the beach and it took me quite a while to reach it, crawling through the brush. Night had almost fallen when I finally bumped into it. I felt my way around, down to a hollow concealed from the beach by a sand berm and thick brush. The hollow was carpeted in green moss. In it stood a little tent made of sticks and goatskins, like an Indian teepee.

I opened a flap and there was Ben Gunn's boat—about as homemade as homemade could be. Goatskins were stretched, hair inside, over a sloppy frame of bent branches lashed with rawhide. It was tiny—small even for someone my size—and I couldn't believe it would float with a full-grown man. It had a low seat across the middle and a crudely carved double-blade paddle, and a coconut shell for a bailer.

If I had to name it, I'd call it a kayak like the Eskimos use, with a pointed stern and bow, though if the Eskimos ever had to depend on Ben Gunn for their boats they'd soon go extinct.

Like any kayak, however, it was light and portable. I could carry it easily with one hand, which gave me my second crazy idea that day. Since I could carry it, what if I were to carry it down to the water and paddle out to the *Hispaniola*? The wise answer was, having cooled off and found the little boat, why not call it a night and go back to my friends in the bunker? That would be sensible. Why would I want to go out to the *Hispaniola*?

Looking back, I realize now that the answer was that the attack had left me feeling useless: Dr. Livesey would have died if she had had to depend on me to save her from the gangster she had shot. There had been nothing I could do to help.

But now I could, because I remembered that when we dropped anchor, the gold-crazed crew had jammed the chain in its locker, forcing Captain Smollett—who would skin me alive if he caught me here—to order the chain removed and a thick rope bent onto the anchor. The knife in my pocket said I could cut that rope and let the ship drift ashore, which ought to throw a monkey wrench into the plans of Long John Silver.

I sat down to wait for the rest of darkness to settle in and ate a great meal of Mounds Bars. The change in the weather was giving me all the breaks. The fog grew thicker and thicker, the night swallowing the last rays of daylight and turning Treasure Island black as the inside of a whale. When I finally picked up the kayak and felt my way down to the beach, there were only two points visible on the entire harbor.

One was a giant fire on the beach beside the swamp where Silver's defeated men were loudly drowning their sorrows. The other was a dim prick of light marking the *Hispaniola*, where they'd stranded her watchmen with no boat of their own. She had swung around her anchor on the ebbing tide, her bow now pointing toward me. The lights I saw were in her cabin, reflected indirectly in the fog.

The tide had been going out for a while. I had to cross the flats, sinking into mud and seaweed. I reached the water's edge, waded out up to my knees, and set the boat down on its keel.

23

Ebb Tide

T HE KAYAK FLOATED high and dry as a leaf. Unfortunately, I soon found out, she also steered like a
leaf. Her favorite direction was sideways, except when she
decided to spin in circles. Even Ben Gunn, Treasure Island's resident naval architect, had admitted, "She's a handful till you figure her out."

It was clear I had not figured her out. She went every way
except the way I wanted to go. Most of the time we floated
broadside to our course. And I don't think I ever would have
made the ship if it weren't for the tide. By good luck, it kept
sweeping me toward the middle of the harbor where the
Hispaniola tugged her anchor.

At first the ship looked like an ink blot on black paper.
Closer, her cabin and radio mast and drooping cannon began
to take shape, somehow blacker than the sky. And then the
tide, which was picking up speed, drove me straight at her
bow. My kayak bumped and slid along her anchor line. I
clapped on, burning my hands on the rough rope, which was
stretched tight as piano wire. I could hear the current pull
the ship against her anchor as it bubbled and rippled past
her hull. One cut with my pocket knife, I thought, and the
Hispaniola would slip away on the tide.

But then I remembered one of the bits of sea lore Long
John had told me. A taut line, suddenly cut, was as danger-

ous as a bucking bronco. Odds were, if I cut it, the snapping ends would throw my kayak and me right out of the water.

That gave me pause, but the weather kept giving me the breaks. The light wind which had been blowing out of the south and southeast had veered around to the southwest. Just as I was about to give up, a strong puff caught the *Hispaniola* and shoved her up against the current, which, to my delight, made the anchor line go slack in my hand.

I whipped out my knife, opened it with my teeth, and sawed away at the thick rope, strand by strand, until only two strands held the ship in place. By then the current had fetched her up again hard on the anchor. I hung on, waiting for another breath of wind to ease the strain.

I could hear shouting in the cabin. One voice I recognized as Israel Hands, Flint's gunner. The other, of course, was Red-cap. Both sounded drunk as skunks, and when they opened a cabin porthole to toss an empty bottle, I realized that they were still going hard at it.

Not only were they drunk, they were also angry, cursing each other, banging fists on the table. The argument died down and they grumbled quietly for a moment, until the next subject rose for discussion, louder and louder, quieting down in turn before words escalated to fists.

On shore, the campfire burned among the trees. Some drunk was singing an endless song with a chorus that rang:

> *"Kill them all, kill them all, kill them all,*
> *The long, the short, and the tall . . ."*

The breeze puffed hard again. The *Hispaniola* crept up her anchor line. The rope grew slack. I sawed with all my might. Long John had taught me to keep my knife always sharp. It severed the last strands like a spider web and the ship was loose.

The kayak bumped into her bow. At the same time the ship began to slowly spin, end for end, across the current.

The looming hull started to drive my little boat under. The way the ship was moving prevented me from shoving off, but I did manage, mightily, to work along the hull back toward the stern. Halfway back, I encountered a light line trailing over the side. I grabbed ahold.

Once I had it in my hands, I used it to pull closer and balance on the tippy kayak for a look into the lighted cabin.

By this time, ship and kayak were making speed. We had already fetched up opposite the campfire and I wondered why the watchmen hadn't noticed. One glance through the porthole told me.

Israel Hands and Red-cap were locked in a deadly embrace, each man gripping the other's throat.

From the beach thundered "The monkeys have no tails in Zamboanga, they were bit off by the whales," while one soul harmonized, "The long, the short, and the tall . . ."

Underfoot, the kayak lurched, changed course, and accelerated. I fell to the bottom, untangled myself, and tried to figure out what was happening. The water was ripply, phosphorescent, and all in motion. A few yards ahead, the *Hispaniola* was rocketing along, me in her wake. She seemed to stagger. Her smokestack and radio mast swayed in the night sky. To my astonishment, she seemed to be wheeling to the south.

I looked over my shoulder and my heart jumped. *Behind* me, *far* behind me and rapidly diminishing, was the campfire. The tidal current had turned at right angles, sweeping the ship, my kayak, and me out the narrow channel into the open sea.

The *Hispaniola* yawed violently, turning twenty degrees. Shouts came from the cabin. I heard feet pounding up the companionway. The drunks had finally stopped fighting in order to see what had gone wrong.

I crouched down low in my miserable little kayak and prayed for a painless death when the breakers at the end of the channel pounded me to pulp and gore. I knew what was coming, I could hear the surf, but I didn't want to look it in the face.

So I huddled there, beaten back and forth by the waves, soaked by spray, waiting for the end. Mercifully, everything sort of shut down inside. I felt tired, weary, ready to sleep. Numbness turned to oblivion, to peace. And so I slept in my little boat, and dreamed of my mother and home.

24

Cruising in My Kayak

I AWAKENED IN broad daylight, bouncing off the southwest coast of Treasure Island. The sun was up, hidden behind the gloomy bulk of Spyglass Hill, which on this side dropped sheer to the sea in monstrous cliffs.

Haulbowline Point and Mizzenmast Hill were right off my side, the hill dark, the point wrapped in cliffs forty or fifty feet high and ringed with ragged masses of fallen rock. I was less than a quarter mile out so I figured to paddle in and land.

I gave that idea up pretty quickly. The breakers blasted into the fallen rocks, spouting spumes of spray, bellowing, thundering as they accelerated toward the shore and burst. It didn't take much imagination to picture the kayak landing like a pebble in a cement mixer. And even if I somehow managed to steer through them, I'd never be able to climb those sheer rock cliffs.

Nor were the cliffs, the surf, and the rocks the only problems, for the rocks were crawling with giant seals—sea lions, I think—huge creatures barking like fiends and hurling their enormous bodies into the water. They had taught me in school that seals didn't hurt people and were really very friendly, but from the perspective of a six-foot goatskin kayak, they looked big and very dangerous. Added all up, starving at sea seemed preferable to attempting a landing on that shore.

And the fact was, I could see a second, better chance coming up. North of Haulbowline Point the land cuts in for a long ways before it sweeps out to another point—the sandy beach, Point of Woods, as it was marked on the chart—covered in tall green pines which come right down to the water.

I remembered that Silver had claimed that the current set northward along the west coast of Treasure Island, and seeing that I was already drifting on it, I figured I'd do much better to try to land on the more hospitable Point of Woods.

There was the usual heavy swell on the sea, but no chop as both the wind and current were coming from the south. Otherwise I'd have drowned, but the smooth surface allowed my little boat to ride the swell with ease. I lay on the bottom and when the swells began to gather like blue whales I would think at first they were about to crash down on me. Instead, the kayak rose with them, bouncing and swaying gently as if it had a mind and heart totally secure that it was born to float forever. Cresting the swell like a bird, we would float gently down the opposite side and the process would start again.

I began to feel brave, so I sat up to have a stab at paddling. But the slightest motion inside the kayak set off a violently magnified reaction. I barely moved my pinky and the kayak immediately rocketed down a steep slope and pounded her nose into the side of the next wave, almost boring through it, and throwing geysers of spray.

Drenched and terrified, I slunk back to my old position, at which point the kayak thanked me by resuming her soft, gentle dance on the surface of the sea. That was good to know, except if it threatened me every time I moved, how was I ever going to paddle it ashore?

I tried to keep my head. First, I very gently bailed the water we had shipped. Then, carefully looking over the gunwale, I tried to figure out what made her float so easily through the rollers.

What I learned was that each wave was actually a series of waves of different size, like a range of hills instead of a single mountain, and the little boat tended to take the easy route, crossing the lower hills by avoiding the steep slopes, crests, and cliffs.

I can do that, I thought. All I had to do was lie still as possible, waiting for a moment when a gentle stroke with the paddle would assist the kayak's progress through the smooth areas and shove it a little toward shore. So I stretched out on my elbows in an incredibly uncomfortable position, and every now and then gave a little poke with the paddle.

It was grim, slow work, but I thought I was gaining ground. Still, the closer we got to the Point of Woods, I realized we would never make it. The waves would sweep the kayak past it a hundred yards offshore. I was close, all right. I could see individual treetops, swaying in the breeze, and thought maybe I'd make the next point.

I'd better, because I was dying of thirst. The sun, blazing from above and reflected by the sea, had dried me out like a dead horseshoe crab. My lips were caked with salt, my throat burning, my brain on fire. I gazed longingly at the green trees as the current swept me past the point. But as I rounded the point and got a look at the next stretch of water, I saw a sight that changed everything.

Right ahead, less than half a mile, I saw the *Hispaniola*.

She looked like she was heading around the island back to the harbor. Seawater frothed white around her bow. "A bone in her teeth," Long John had taught me, indicated that a ship was making speed. That meant it was only a matter of minutes until Israel Hands spotted me and hauled me aboard or ran me over, but I was so thirsty that I didn't know whether to be happy or sad.

In a while, though, I realized there was no smoke pouring

from her stack. Then the "bone" subsided and she began to drop off, showing me less of her bow and more of her sides.

She was rolling, rolling clumsily. I wondered if the helmsmen had fallen asleep, but soon it was apparent she was not making way. She began to sweep in my direction, and I figured they'd spotted me, but she fell away again.

Now I saw a thin wisp of smoke from the stack—thin as a thread. Puzzled, I came to the gradual conclusion that her rudder was tied, and she was engaged "ahead" with the engine ticking over just enough to hold her to the seas. If I could sit up and paddle and not capsize I just might intercept her.

A dream of a cool drink in her galley made me brave. I immediately took spray, but I kept at it, carefully paddling toward the *Hispaniola*. Once I shipped such a sea that I had to stop and bail, but I got better at paddling and steering as the chase went on. I was gaining. I could see the spokes of the helm through the wheelhouse glass, one of them secured by a loop of rope as I had guessed.

But I saw no one on deck. Hands and Red-cap were sleeping it off, I figured, having tied the helm in drunken hopes of keeping her off the rocks. Not the brightest of moves, to be sure, but few of Silver's men, as he himself had noted, put much effort into thinking. If I could catch up and somehow get aboard, I could batten down the hatches and lock them below while they were still sleeping.

It was slow going. A couple of times I thought she was just going to fall off a wave, turn around, and steam away, but each time she came up again, almost as if she was looking for a friend. I'll be your friend, I promised. Just let me aboard. My head was dancing with thirst. I began hallucinating visions of a tall pitcher of iced tea in the fridge.

At last I got my shot. A big wave carried me to its crest. The kayak skidded down it and smack against the *Hispaniola*'s hull. My rejoicing was brief. The ship rose and plunged like a demented elevator, a wall of steel pounding in and out of the sea a foot from my face. The kayak nearly slid under her. When it rose, I saw my chance, leaped at the apogee of the kayak's flight, and flung my arms over the *Hispaniola*'s bulwark. I smacked my jaw so hard I saw stars and began to fall.

Kicking down to push off the kayak, I felt the little goat-skin boat shudder under a heavy blow. The ship drove the kayak under, and with it any chance of retreating from the *Hispaniola*.

25

Captain Hawkins

ONE OF MY guns fell in the water as I dived a desperate half gainer over the bulwark and flopped headfirst on the *Hispaniola*'s filthy deck. You have crazy thoughts at scary moments. Mine was, Boy, wait till Captain Smollett sees this! Crusted with chewing gum and cigarette butts, the decks hadn't been swabbed since the mutiny broke out. An empty bottle, broken off at the neck, rolled and banged in the scuppers.

Though it appeared that I was alone, I could feel the engine grinding far below. I climbed cautiously to the wheelhouse. Halfway there, on the fiddley deck—the railed space on the cabin roof, one flight below the wheelhouse—I found my shipmates.

Red-cap lay on his back, stiff as a board. His arms were spread wide like a crucifix. His teeth grinned through his open lips like yellow piano keys. Propped against the railing beside him lay Israel Hands. His chin was on his chest, his face as white as chalk. Blood spattered the deck around them and it looked as if they had killed each other in a drunken brawl.

The ship kept up her bronco bucking, slamming into the seas, back and forth as the loosely tied rudder slipped from side to side. It occurred to me that maybe one of them was still alive, because the ship couldn't have held her head to the waves very long. Someone had tied her recently.

Certainly not Red-cap. At every jump his body rolled. But—awful to see—nothing altered the position of his frozen limbs or his grotesque grin. At each jump, too, Hands seemed to sink deeper into himself, lower and lower onto the deck, his feet sliding farther out, his body angling sternward.

While I was watching and wondering, Hands rolled half over and, groaning, dragged himself back into a half-sitting position. It was a groan of pain and serious injury, and the way his jaw sagged made me feel sorry for him for a second. Then I remembered what I had overheard in the pistachio barrel, especially the things he had said about Dr. Livesey. I walked toward him and stopped, just out of reach.

"Is it your watch, Mr. Hands?" I asked sarcastically.

His eyes rolled heavily toward me, but he was too far gone to show surprise. All he had the strength to say was "Brandy."

The ship lurched again and he slid, revealing under his leg the gun he had dropped after shooting Red-cap. I eased closer, knelt, and snapped it away in a flash. It was a little revolver, what poor Tom Redruth had called a belly gun. I stashed it in my belt, glad of a friend to replace the one I'd dropped.

"Brandy," Israel moaned again, reminding me that I too was thirsty and starving and didn't have time to play games. I ran down to the cabin.

They had wrecked it. Every locker had been smashed open in hunts for the chart and booze. They'd tracked swamp mud all over the floor, and every white surface was smeared by dirty hands. Empty bottles filled the corners, clinking as the ship rolled. One of Dr. Livesey's medical books lay on the table, opened to a section called Female Anatomy.

Foraging through the garbage, I lucked out and found

some of Captain Smollett's Fig Newtons, raisins, and a brick of Velveeta cheese with toothmarks on the end. I took a long drink of water. It was horribly warm, since some idiot had left the refrigerator open, but I drank until I could swallow no more, and took a jar up on deck to sip from while I ate.

Israel had discovered a pint bottle somewhere. He drained it in one long gurgle. "Son of a bitch, I needed that!"

I sat down at a safe distance, cut away the gnawed end, and began to eat the cheese. "How badly are you hurt?"

He grunted. "If that doc was aboard, I'd be fit as a fiddle. Bad luck is what's wrong with me." He glanced at Red-cap, lurching stiffly beside him. "Bastard's dead. Dumb lubber, what did he expect? So how about you? Where'd you come from, kid?"

"I came to take over the ship. You can call me Captain, Mr. Hands."

Hands did not look pleased, nor did he seem to see any humor in my statement. The drink had put some color back in his weathered cheeks, but he still looked sick as a dog, and couldn't keep from slipping every time the ship lurched. Watching me closely now, he finally spoke. "I suppose, Captain Hawkins, you might want to get ashore."

"I might," I admitted.

"Maybe we ought to have a little talk."

"Talk," I said, trying to sound as sure and unconcerned as Captain Smollett had when Long John Silver came waving his white flag. I sat down and popped some cheese and raisins in my mouth.

"This guy," Israel said, nodding feebly at the salvage diver's corpse, "his name was O'Brien—a dumb Mick— cranked up her main engine, intending for us to conn her back to the harbor. Now he's dead. How you going to sail her in alone?"

"O'Brien did the hard part, starting the engine. I can steer by myself."

"All the way around to the harbor?"

"I'm not going near that harbor. I'm going to beach her inside North Inlet."

Israel studied me with a bleary eye. "Excellent move. Exactly what I would do in your position. Only how you going to get her inside? That channel's about six inches wider than this ship. You need help. I'll make you a deal. You get me some food and a little more to drink and patch up where that bastard stuck me and I'll lead you inside that narrow little harbor."

"Why would you help me?"

"Hey, you won, kid. I've had it. I'm hurt bad. I got to help you."

This made sense. He needed food and nursing. And if I wrecked the ship trying to bring her in alone, he'd drown with me. So I said okay. I ran below and got an old scarf my mother had given me in case it got cold. Hands used it to tie up a deep, bleeding stab in his thigh.

Eating some cheese and raisins after that, and slugging back some water, he perked up considerably. "Feel like a new man," he said. "Mighty grateful. It takes a real gent to be kind to his vanquished foe."

I carried a milk carton up to the wheelhouse and in a glow of victory, turned the ship around and headed her north at six knots. I thought I had made up for running away and deserting my friends. The *Hispaniola* kited along in the bright sunshine. Soon we passed the highlands and stretches of low, sandy beaches. Then we turned the northern corner of the rocky cliffs.

I still felt pretty good, except I didn't like the way Israel Hands was watching me. He had a funny little smile floating on his face. It was partly a tired old man's smile, crooked with pain and weakness. But I wondered, when he dragged himself up to the wheelhouse, complaining of the hot sun, if I saw more than pain and weakness in his expression—contempt perhaps, or even treachery, as he watched and watched and watched me steer the ship.

26

Israel Hands

T HE T I D E H A D just started rising when we reached the mouth of the North Inlet. Israel told me we would have to wait an hour before it filled the channel deep enough to accommodate our draft. I stopped a mile offshore and, under the coxswain's guidance, tied the wheel. When I finally got her turning in low, lazy circles, we sat back and made a lunch of the rest of the cheese.

"Captain?" he said after a while, with that same mysterious smile, "what do you say you deep-six my old pal O'-Brien? I ain't usually squeamish—it weren't my fault I had to kill him in self-defense—but he's beginning to stink."

"I'm not strong enough and I sure don't want to touch him."

"This is a bad-luck ship, Jim. A heap of guys been killed on the old *Hispaniola*—can't even count how many since we left New York. I never seen such bad luck. Now O'Brien . . . O'Brien's dead, ain't he? Hell, I'm just a dumb swabbie, but you been to school. You read and write. Tell me something. Is he dead for good or will he suddenly come alive again?"

"My mother says dead people go to heaven."

"Jeez. If that's true, then killing them is a waste of time. Well, I'm not afraid of ghosts and I don't suppose you are either. Listen kid, would you get me a—jeez, I can't think straight—get me a beer, huh? That brandy made my head spin."

I smelled a rat. The coxswain's confusion seemed about as genuine as his sudden desire to discuss the philosophy of ghosts. Nor did I believe that he preferred beer to brandy. I figured he wanted me out of the way for a minute. He wouldn't meet my eye, glancing out the windows or down at O'Brien's body on the fiddley deck. And he kept smiling that sneery smile. I figured to play along to see what he was up to, so I said, "You want a beer? Any particular brand?"

"Well, you probably won't find any beer down there. Anyhow it'll be warm. How about a bottle of rum? I think I saw one stashed behind the fridge. Long John's private stock. I wouldn't mind a sip of that."

"Okay, I'll find you some rum. It'll take me a few minutes. You guys really made a mess of the place."

With that, I went pounding noisily down the interior companionway. Then I took off my shoes and snuck quietly to a porthole where I could see the outside stairs.

Sure enough, here came Israel, moving pretty spryly for a man with a wounded leg, though he did groan and bite his lips. He crept across the fiddley deck, reached under O'-Brien's corpse, and came up with a double-bladed knife long enough to butcher a hog. It was bloodstained to the hilt. I figured it was the one O'Brien had stuck in Israel's thigh before Israel shot him. Israel hid it inside his shirt and climbed back up to the wheelhouse.

Not a pretty picture. First of all, Israel could move about. Now he was armed. And since he'd gone to the trouble of tricking me to go below, it was pretty clear who he had in mind for his next victim. I had no idea what he intended to do after he killed me, whether he planned to crawl all the way across the island from North Inlet to the swamps, or hoped his friends would somehow come and get him.

There was only one thing I could count on: we needed each other, for the moment. He knew he wasn't strong enough to run the ship all the way around the island alone. So we needed each other to conn her into the shelter of the inlet. Until we had her securely on the beach, I was safe, I hoped.

While convincing myself of this, I put on my shoes and hurried down to the galley, found the stashed rum, and carried the bottle back to the wheelhouse.

Israel Hands sat where I had left him, huddled up on a corner stool where he could watch the wheel and the circling sea. His eyes were closed, as if too weak to stand the light. But he looked up at my arrival, unscrewed the bottle cap, and took a deep swig with his favorite toast, "To my old boss, Captain Flint. Luck!" He slumped down awhile, then fished a pack of Camels from his pocket. "Got a light, Jim? Give me a match, will you, kid? Figure I got strength for one more coffin nail. Oh boy, what a way to go, far from home, with my boots on . . ."

"I'll give you a light, but if I were you, I'd be saying my prayers."

"Why bother?"

"Why bother? You were the one just asking about what happens when we die. You've broken every rule in the Bible. There's the last man you killed, lying right there. And you wonder why you ought to pray? How about for mercy?"

I was practically yelling at him, thinking of the knife he'd hidden and how he planned to use it on me. But Israel took another deep swig of rum and answered me as solemnly as an old uncle sharing his deepest thoughts over a cup of coffee.

"Thirty years I been at sea. I seen good and bad, better and worse, flat calms and typhoons, grub running low, knives flashing, you name it. But I never seen good come of goodness yet. Hit 'em before they hit you, kid. Shoot first, ask questions later; dead men don't bite. That's the way it goes, kid. Dead men don't bite."

Suddenly he changed his tone. "Enough talk. Tide's in. Okay, Captain Hawkins, you just obey orders and we'll put her on the beach."

It was a tricky two miles because the entrance to the little harbor was both narrow and shallow. I took the wheel and did exactly what he told me and Hands proved to be a crackerjack pilot. We entered the channel as neat as a piston in a cylinder.

The instant we were inside, the land closed around us. The shores were as jungly as the southern anchorage, but the fairway was longer and narrower, really no wider than a river, which it was, lacking the broad pond of Captain Kidd's anchorage. Basically we sailed over a bar and right up the mouth of the river.

And in case we were wondering if we needed each other's help, there at the narrow end lay the remains of a wrecked ship—an enormous rusty hull.

"Tore her bottom on the bar," muttered Israel. It looked like it had been there for many years, all rusty and dripping in seaweed and studded with barnacles. It had fallen onto one side, and trees and flowering shrubs were growing on its deck.

"Heads up," said Israel. "Ease in alongside of her. See that smooth sand, not even a cat's-paw on the water. Dead calm. Just run her up on there, easy."

"How do we get her off again?"

"Take a line ashore on the other side, bend it around one of them big pine trees, back around the capstan and crank her off at high tide. Stand by. She's got too much way on her. Back engine. A little stern power. Little more—steady—starboard helm. Steady!"

He gave his orders, cool and clear. I scrambled between wheel and throttle and gear lever, trying to shove the little bits I had learned into this one moment. Suddenly he cried, "Hard aport!"

Concentrating on this maneuver, I failed to keep a close

eye on Israel. Now, as the ship drifted the last several yards, bow on toward the beach, I craned to see out the window. I might have died where I stood, clutching the helm, if a funny feeling hadn't suddenly made me turn my head. I might have heard the deck creak or maybe I caught a glimpse of his shadow. Maybe it was just the instinct of any hunted creature. Whatever, when I turned, I saw Israel coming fast with his knife in his hand.

We both yelled when our eyes met, me with a shrill cry of terror, he an angry roar like a charging lion. He lunged. I was trapped between the wheel and the port side of the wheelhouse. I jumped sideways, releasing the wheel; the rudder, locked hard over in our last turn, spun back to starboard. The spokes, spinning in a blur, clipped Israel lightly on the jaw, which stopped him for a brief second.

Before he recovered, I escaped from the corner he had backed me into, and raced for the back door of the wheelhouse, hoping to get out of the confined space. He got there first. I pulled the belly gun, cocked it and aimed, and when he lunged again, pulled the trigger. All I got was a tiny "click" like a marble falling on the sidewalk.

"Empty, kid," Israel said, smiling. "Used my last on O'-Brien."

I threw it at him. He ducked with a cackly laugh that faded when I pulled my own gun from my jacket.

Wounded as he was, it was amazing how fast Israel could move. He roared again, his filthy gray hair flying in his blood-red face, red with fury and murder. He tore after me out the door and blocked the stairs, trapping me again between the wheelhouse and the railing.

I aimed and fired. Another "click."

The long wet night in the kayak had soaked the gun. I steadied myself with a hand on the radio mast and tried to figure out what to do next. He slashed at me with the knife. I parried with the gun and he backhanded it, almost knocking it out of my fingers.

I faked toward the door, hoping to jump for the ladder. Seeing I was trying to dodge, he stopped and again we dueled, his bloodstained knife against my useless gun. It was sort of like playing tag at home, jumping around the breakwaters on the beach, only winning for him would mean steel in my guts. It was a kid's game, though, and I could probably outmaneuver an old seaman for quite a while. That made me a little braver, until I realized that in the end he still held the knife.

Suddenly the *Hispaniola* ground her bow into the sand. She staggered, pushed farther ashore, and just as suddenly fell on her side, skidding both me and Israel Hands across the deck like a pair of bowling pins. Her deck was canted at a steep angle. We tumbled into the rails and the next second dead O'Brien joined us, arms spread wide and stiff as a frame of two-by-fours.

Trapped between them, I cracked my head on Israel's boot so hard it rattled my teeth. Fortunately, he got tangled up in O'Brien and even though my head was ringing, I was first on my feet and running for the radio mast before I had time to think.

Speed saved me again. Israel's knife screeched a gouge out of the wood, six inches below my foot as I scrambled up the mast. He gaped up at me, his face a cartoon of disappointment and rage.

I broke open my revolver and shook the bullets from the cylinder. I dried them on my shirt and blew the seawater out of the chambers and the hammer, paying close attention to the firing pin. Israel, noting this, put his knife between his teeth and started up the steeply slanting mast.

With less than eight feet separating us, I quickly reloaded and snicked the cylinder shut. "One more step, Mr. Hands, and I'll blow your head off. Dead men don't bite, remember?"

Israel stopped and took the knife from his teeth. "You think drying your bullets is going to make a difference?"

"Want to bet?" I asked, taking aim.

Clearly, he didn't want to chance it.

"Jim," he said. "Looks like you got the drop on me. I'd have nailed you to the bulkhead if she hadn't run aground at that exact goddamned moment. You got all the luck. I never get any luck. I'm the unluckiest son of a bitch you'll ever meet. So, anyhow, I gotta surrender. That's all there is to it. I give up, which is a bitch for an old sailor like me to give up to a wet-behind-the-ears kid like you."

I felt great. I was listening and smiling and celebrating how I'd get back to my friends a hero, when suddenly his right hand flicked back over his shoulder. Something buzzed through the air. I felt a hard blow and needle-sharp pain and the next I knew I couldn't move.

My shoulder was pinned to the mast. In the second it took to realize he had thrown the knife—a second of horrid pain and belly-ripping fear—I had pulled the trigger. The little gun bucked right out of my hand and fell. It didn't fall alone. Israel screamed, let go of the mast to clutch his heart, and dropped headfirst into the harbor.

27

"Pieces of Eight"

THE *HISPANIOLA* LAY at such an angle that I could look straight down into the water from my perch atop the radio mast. Israel Hands, not as far up the mast as I, had been nearer to the ship, but his body still cleared the hull. He struggled to the surface, bubbling blood, splashing around. Then the water closed over his head again, and he sank like a stone. As the ripples died, I could see his body spread out on the sandy bottom. He twitched a little as fish flitted by, but he was dead—shot and drowned—lunch for the same barracudas he had tried to feed with me.

I was sick, faint and scared silly. Hot blood ran down my back and chest. His knife, where it had pinned my shoulder to the mast, burned like hot needles. But worse, far worse, than the pain was my fear of falling from the mast into the water beside Israel's body.

I shut my eyes so I couldn't see him and held on with all my might until my fingers ached. It felt like I clung there for hours, instead of the minutes it must have been. Finally, gradually, I calmed down enough to try to think my way down to solid ground.

First, I tried to pull the knife out of the mast. But either it was in too deep or I lost my nerve. Shaking from head to toe, I gave it up. In a weird way, I think, that shudder saved me. Israel's knife had come very close to missing me completely; in fact, I was pinned to the mast by only a thin sliver of skin, and when I shook, it tore and I was loose. There was blood all over the place, but the only thing that held me now was my jacket. I tore that away too and shinnied down the mast to the slanting deck.

I staggered below, washed the blood off, then searched the empties until I found one with an inch of rum still swirling in the bottom. I knew I wasn't going to enjoy what I had to do, but I remembered Dr. Livesey's warnings about infections on the island. I closed my eyes, bit my lips, and poured the rum on my neck. It stung so bad I dropped the bottle and jumped around the cabin trying not to cry. When I finally caught my breath, I found the bleeding had stopped. I could even use my arm a little.

Up on deck I had a look around the ship—mine, now, except for the dead O'Brien roasting in the sun. I decided he had to go. He was about as horrible-looking a shipmate as you could ask for, leaning against the bulwark with his arms and legs at odd angles like a life-size Howdy Doody with his strings cut. All the color had drained from his face, so his once suntanned skin looked as gray and translucent as waxed paper. Before I had sailed to Treasure Island I wouldn't have touched his body with a ten-foot pole. As it was, I had seen so much death and agony in the last two days that one more dead body wasn't that big a deal.

I grabbed his belt, planted my feet, and worked him up the slanted bulwark and tipped him into the water. He splashed like a heavy anchor and went straight to the bottom, where he landed across old Israel with his bald head on the killer's knee. His red cap remained on the surface, floating above the barracudas who returned to investigate.

Alone, at last.

The sun was setting, so low that the pines cast shadows that crossed the anchorage and darkened my decks. The evening land breeze accompanied the shadows. The twin-peak hill to the east protected the shelter to some extent, but it made me wonder how the beached ship would handle a hard blow or a storm tide. She would lie more and more on her beam ends as the tide ran out, and I could only hope that she would rise with the next one coming in. I figured the right thing to do was close all her watertight hatches, the big deck hatches and the several doors and portholes in the house. When I was done, she was secure as a submarine, all the way up to the wheelhouse.

By now the entire anchorage was in shadow except for a single beam of sunlight that lit the flowering weeds on the wrecked ship next to mine. It started getting cold.

I went up to the bow and had a look at the water. Pretty shallow. I swung over the bulkhead and shinnied down the cut anchor rope. The water was barely up to my waist and I waded ashore on clean white sand. Turning back for a last look at my ship, I saw the sun drop below the horizon. The wind worked lower in the trees.

I felt great, back on dry land, with a ship to show for it. Silver's men would never find her, but when my friends were ready to leave Treasure Island we could winch her off the beach just the way the coxswain explained. All I had to do now was walk across the island home to the bunker and tell everybody what a hero I was. I figured whatever trouble I was in for sneaking off would be more than made up by my capturing the ship. (With a lot of luck, maybe even Captain Smollett would see it that way.)

So I headed inland, picturing the chart I had studied a thousand times. I remembered that the easternmost of the rivers that drained into Captain Kidd's anchorage started from the foot of the twin-peaked hill on the left. My best bet would be to cross that river while it was still a narrow stream. The woods were fairly open and I made good time. Sticking close to the ridge that formed the base of the hill, I waded the young river where it didn't even come up to my knees.

This brought me close to where I'd met Ben Gunn. I

walked cautiously now, keeping a sharp eye. The dusk had darkened sky and treetops and there was little to see, but as I reached a point where I could see between the two peaks I noticed a flickering glow against the sky, which I figured was the goat-man cooking supper on a roaring fire. I was surprised he'd be so open. If I could see his fire, what about Silver and his gang camped in the marsh?

The night got black. I had to navigate by the fading gloom of the double hill behind me and Spyglass on my right. There were few stars, too dim to cast any light. I started tripping over bushes and falling into holes.

Suddenly it got brighter. I looked up and saw moonbeams glinting on the top of Spyglass. Then the moon itself rose round and silvery among the trees. I could hardly believe that the same moon, three or four nights ago, had found me in the pistachio barrel. But as Long John Silver used to say when we were scrubbing pots, "Time flies when you're having fun."

With the moon to help me see I made good time, walking fast among the trees, running across the grassy meadows. Only when I neared the woods around the bunker did I slow down to travel softly and quietly. I certainly didn't want to get shot by mistake by my own friends.

I finally got to the edge of the clearing. The western end was bathed in moonlight. The rest, and the bunker itself, were still in black shadow, streaked with silver beams. On the other side of the bunker an enormous fire had burned down to embers that emitted a steady red glow, which appeared almost solid in contrast to the airy moonlight. I couldn't see a soul. Nor was there a sound, except the breeze.

I stopped, puzzled and a little scared. We didn't build such big fires. Captain Smollett was at his worst on the subject of wasting firewood. I began to get an awful feeling that something had gone badly wrong while I was away.

I sneaked around the eastern end, sticking to the shadows, and slipped through the barbed wire where it was so dark I couldn't see my own hand.

Then, still not taking any chances, I got down on my hands and knees and crawled silent as a snake. Suddenly, as I got near the bunker, I heard a sound that almost made me laugh with relief. It's not a pretty sound—sometimes it will drive you crazy—but at that moment, crawling with my heart in my mouth, I was the happiest guy in the Caribbean to hear the noise of my friends snoring. The soft warm voice of my mother whispering "Sleep tight" never sounded more reassuring.

One thing was for sure, they kept a lousy watch. What if I were Long John and his boys creeping in to slit their throats? That was the worst thing about having Captain Smollett wounded, I thought, feeling guilty again for leaving them—no one to maintain discipline. And of course my leaving left them short of hands to stand guard.

I stood up and peeked in the door. It was pitch dark inside and I couldn't see a thing. All I could hear was the snoring and an occasional clicking noise I couldn't place.

Feeling my way in the dark, I walked into the bunker slowly, softly, and headed for my own blankets. I couldn't wait to see their faces when they woke up and found me in the morning. I covered my mouth to stifle a laugh.

I kicked something soft—a sleeper's leg. I stopped dead. But he just turned and groaned and resumed snoring.

Then all of a sudden a shrill scream shattered the silence:

"Pieces of eight! Pieces of eight! Pieces of eight! Pieces of eight!" and on and on and on, longer and louder than a Pontiac assembly line.

Long John's parrot, Captain Flint. It was she making the clicking noise, pecking at a piece of bark. She, standing watch better than any human could, announcing my arrival with her miserable shrieking.

I was caught totally off balance. The sleepers jumped up, awake and cursing. Silver cursed the loudest, bellowing "Who the hell is there?"

I turned to run, bounced off one guy and straight into the arms of another, who smothered me in a combination hammerlock and chokehold.

"Bring a light, Dick," ordered Silver.

A flashlight blazed in my face.

PART SIX

CAPTAIN SILVER

28

In the Enemy Camp

T HE FLASHLIGHT AND a bunch of burning sticks brought from the fire lit up the bunker and showed me how completely the tables had turned. Silver's gang had the bunker and all our food and drink.

But worse, no prisoners. All my friends were dead. Scared as I was—and I was shaking—I kept wishing I had stayed. One more gun reloaded, one machete passed, might have made the difference.

There were six of the gang left. Five were on their feet, cursing and grumbling, their faces swollen, just dragged out of a drunken sleep. The sixth, badly wounded, with a bloody bandage on his head, could only prop himself up on one elbow, pale and cursing faintly. I figured he was the one who'd been shot trying to scale the wire in the big attack and had run back to the woods.

The parrot sat preening her feathers on Long John's shoulder. Heroine of the moment, she watched me with a cold, cold vulture's eye and I wondered how many men and boys she'd seen die in her two hundred years.

Long John himself looked pale and grim. He still wore his fancy captain's coat, but it was a mess, missing brass buttons, smeared with mud, and torn by briars. His face was blank as a tombstone, his eyes bleak, his mouth thinner than a razor.

"Well, if it isn't Jim Hawkins. Happened to be in the neighborhood, Jim? Dropped in to say hello? Mighty friendly. Mighty friendly . . . So, how you doing, kid?"

He sat down on one of the ammunition boxes. "Give me a light, Dick." He got his cigarette going, blew some smoke. "Sit down, boys. Might as well get back in the sack. No need to stand for Mr. Hawkins. He'll excuse you. Won't you, Jim? Okay, so here you are. A real nice surprise. I knew you were smart first time I saw you, but this elevates you to splendid new heights."

I couldn't figure out where he was going, so I said nothing. They had backed me against the wall. I worked hard at looking Silver in the face, hoping to seem unconcerned, but I was Jell-O inside.

Silver blew some more smoke.

"Thing is, Jim, since you're here, I've got to tell you how things stand. I've always liked you, kid. You got balls. Remind me of myself when I was your age. I always wanted you to join us and take your share and be one of the guys. . . .

"Well, kid, now's your chance. Your last chance. Captain Smollett's a fine seaman, but a ball-buster. He goes by the book, so you better steer clear of him. And your pal the lady doctor, she's had it with you, son. 'Ungrateful little—' Well, you can fill in the word she used. So what it comes down to is, you can't go back. Your old pals won't have you since you ran away. So unless you intend to start a third ship's company all by yourself, which might get lonely, you gotta join with me."

I thought, Thank God, at least my friends are still alive, somewhere on the island. Of course that wasn't doing me a lot of good at the moment, while *his* friends watched me from the shadows with eyes that glowed like cats'.

"Now I'm not making a threat," Silver continued, "though you are, of course, in our, shall we say, control.

You're welcome to join up. If you don't want to, you're free to say no. Fair enough?"

"Can I ask you something?" I said in a very shaky voice. All his sneering sarcasm told me that death was circling like a gull. My cheeks were burning and my heart was pounding like a jackhammer.

"Ask anything you want, Jim. Think it over. No one's pushing you. No hurry. We got all the time in the world for a nice guy like you."

"Well," I said, feeling a little braver, "if I have to choose, it would help to know what's up. Why are you here and where did my friends go?"

"You want to know what's up?" growled Morgan. "You're what's up."

"Pipe down!" snapped Silver. He turned back to me in his seemingly gentle way. "Yesterday morning, Mr. Hawkins, Dr. Livesey came waving a truce flag.

" 'You've had it, Silver,' she said, 'your ship's gone.'

"Well, maybe we had a drink or two last night. Maybe a few too many. At any rate, no one had looked out. And son of a bitch, the doc was right, the ship was gone.

" 'Okay,' says La Doc-sie, 'let's make a deal.'

"And that's just what we did, Jim. Worked out a trade. We got the food and booze, the bunker and the firewood you were so kind to cut. The whole shooting match, as it were."

"What about my friends?"

"In return, we let them go. They skedaddled. I don't know where."

He dragged deep on his cigarette.

"In case you're wondering where you fit in the treaty, here's what's up: 'How many to leave?' I asked the doc.

" 'Four,' said the doc. 'Four, including one wounded.'

" 'What about the kid? What about Jim Hawkins?' I asked.

" 'I don't know where he is and I couldn't care less,' she said. 'We've had it with his running away.' Sorry, Jim. That's what she said."

"Is that all?" I asked.

"That's all."

"And I'm supposed to choose?"

"Right this minute."

I could be sarcastic too, I thought. Nothing to lose. "The thing is, ever since I met you, people have been dying right and left. So I don't think you're offering me a really great choice, Mr. Silver. But there's things you oughta know."

"Yeah, what?"

"First of all, you're in a lot of trouble."

"*I'm* in a lot of trouble?" he asked, and his men sort of chuckled.

"Yeah, you. You lost your ship. You lost the treasure. You lost most of your men. And your whole plan is ruined. You want to know why?" I got excited, and all of a sudden I wasn't afraid. If I was going down anyway, I might as well go down in flames. "I'll tell you why. 'Cause of me. I was in the pistachio barrel the night we sighted land. I heard you, John, and Dick Johnson, and Hands—who's fish food right now—and I repeated every word to the senator, the captain, and the doctor. And who do you think cut the ship's anchor line? Me. And who do you think fed Israel Hands to the fish? Me. The joke's on you, Silver. I've been on top since the beginning. I'm not afraid of you. Kill me, if you want. But I'll promise you this: if you let me go, I won't hold any grudges. And when you're on trial for mutiny and piracy and murder, I'll do everything I can to help you. So *you've* got a choice: another killing, or a witness to save you from the electric chair."

They just sat there, staring at me like sheep, until I ran out of breath.

"I'll keep it in mind," Silver said.

I couldn't tell whether he was laughing at me or actually thinking it over.

Then Morgan shouted, "That isn't all he did! He was the one who knew Black Dog."

"No shit, Sherlock," said Long John Silver. "He's also the one that stole the chart from Billy Bones. Fact is, every time we've run aground it's been Jim Hawkins's fault."

"Somebody oughta slit his throat and stick his leg through it," roared Morgan. He flicked a switchblade from his back pocket.

"Hold it!" snapped Silver. "Who the hell appointed you captain? You want to slit throats, you clear it with me first."

Tom lowered his knife, but the others took up his protest.

"Tom's right," said one.

"I been pushed around enough," added another. "I'm done taking crap from you, Silver."

"You guys looking for trouble with *me?*" roared Silver. "Buck me and you'll join a long line of corpses. Thirty years I been putting guys in line—knife, gun, fists, whatever it took. No one ever crossed me that had a happy day after. I'll be goddamned if I let some illiterate swabbie push me around in my 'declining' years. You want to fight?" He drew deep on his cigarette and looked each sailor in the face. "Grab a knife and I'll spill your guts on the deck before I finish my smoke. Step up, boys. Don't be shy."

No one spoke a word. No one moved an inch.

"What a pack of heroes. Now hear this, heroes! I'm captain. You elected me captain. And I'm captain because I can kick your asses. You will obey, dead or alive." Long John Silver inhaled another lungful of smoke. "Get this straight: I like this boy. I never seen a better kid in my life. He happens to be more man than any two of you wharf rats. So put away your blade, Tom Morgan, and don't let me catch anyone even looking cross-eyed at the kid."

Back to the wall, heart pounding, I sensed a glimmer of

hope. Silver waited, cigarette dangling from his lip, eye cocked against the smoke as calm as if he were baking pies in his galley. Yet his eyes were everywhere, warily tracking his gang. They were whispering and shuffling their feet, gradually retreating toward the door. Muttering, hissing, faces red in the light from the burning sticks, they shot murderous glances our way. Not at me, but at Silver himself.

"You boys seem to have a lot on your minds," Silver remarked. "Speak up loud and clear, or shut up."

"Trouble is, sir," answered a tall, hard-looking, yellow-eyed sailor, "you're playing pretty fast and loose with the rules. We don't like being pushed around. We got rights. Like you said, we elected you. We got a right to talk it over."

And snapping him a salute, the sailor sauntered coolly out the door, trailed by his mates. Each gave Silver a salute, and an excuse. "Just following the rules, sir." "We got our rights, sir." "Sorry, sir." They all marched out, leaving me alone with Silver.

The second they were gone, he ground out his cigarette.

"Listen up, Jim," he whispered. "You're about one minute from death, and about thirty seconds from torture, which is worse. A lot worse. They're going to elect a new captain. But don't worry, I'll stand by you through thick and thin. I wasn't going to, not until you spoke up. But I realized you're a solid guy I can count on, like you can count on me. I said to myself, You stand by Hawkins and Hawkins'll stand by you. Hawkins is my last card and I'm his last card too. We'll fight 'em back to back, Jim. You save your witness, I told myself, and he'll save you from the hot seat."

I began to see where he was heading. "In other words, you're giving up on the gold."

"Unconditional surrender," he answered. "No choice. Ship gone, I'm finished. Once I looked into that bay, Jim, and saw no *Hispaniola*— Sure I'm tough, but I can't do the impossible."

I was bewildered. "Impossible" was exactly the way I saw things now. He'd been the leader all along. Now he was surrendering and asking me to join him. I had no choice but to say, "I'll do what I can."

"Now you're talking, pal. You got a deal. And I got a chance."

Happily, he lit up a new cigarette from a burning stick. I could see by its red flame that he was feeling lucky again.

"Nobody ever said I was dumb. I'm on the senator's side now, one of your boys. I know you hid the ship somewhere. I can tell. How you did it, Lord knows. I guess Hands and O'Brien pulled some dumb stunt—neither of them could tell shit from Shinola. I ain't asking any questions. What you did was your business. But I know when the jig is up. And I know a solid kid when I see one. Solid and *young!* Jeez, Jim, the scams we could of pulled together."

He poured some rum from a bottle into a tin cup.

"Drink, pal?"

"No thanks. Pal."

"Well, I could sure use a snort. We got trouble heading our way on all four feet. And speaking of trouble, Jim, why'd La Doc-sie give me the chart?"

"Dr. Livesey gave you the chart?" I blurted in amazement. If my words didn't reveal my astonishment, my face must have. Anyway, that finished his questions, though he looked as if my confusion had greatly added to his.

"She sure did. I guess she knew what she was up to. Whatever, good or bad."

And he slugged back the rum, shaking his big blond head like a man expecting the worst.

29

The Black Ballots

Tʜᴇ ɢᴀɴɢ sᴛʀᴏᴅᴇ back into the bunker, their faces dark.

By the way they couldn't look at me I knew that the vote had gone against Long John Silver and that I was as good as dead. George, their leader, waved a fistful of folded papers.

"We've voted," he announced. "Secret ballot so each of us could vote his conscience. You want to count the result?" He thrust them at Silver.

"How'd you happen to find paper out in the jungle?" asked Silver.

"Tore it off a book Dick had. Quit stalling. Count 'em."

Silver inspected the ballots by the light of the torch, without opening them. "Black's a funny color for a book," he remarked innocently. He showed me. Indeed, the papers were black.

"Know what I think, Dick?" Silver asked.

"No, John. What?"

"Quit stalling!"

"I'll bet old George here tore the fly leaves outta your Bible."

Silver, as usual, had read his man right. Dick blustered, "Yeah, so?"

"Well, back when I was growing up, desecrating a Bible was considered bad luck. Damned bad luck."

"Bull!" said George.

"I told you not to cut my Bible," whined Dick.

"Well, what's done is done," shrugged Silver. "Who gave it to you? Your mother?"

"How'd you know, John?"

"Shuddup!" yelled George. "John, you got to count the ballots."

"Sure you trust me?"

"Don't worry, I'll have a look when you're done. Count 'em."

"Okay, okay. Let me see 'em by the light here. Now where in hell did I put my glasses—oh, yeah, forgot, lost 'em in the swamp. Jim, you want to read these to me?"

" 'Deposed,' " I read from the first. He opened the others, one by one, and one by one I read, " 'Deposed.' "

"Well, that's that," said George, who didn't seem all that surprised by the outcome of the secret vote. "Time to elect a new captain."

"Not so fast," said Silver. "Who's forgetting the rules now? You can't vote a guy out before you read the charges against him and give him a chance to defend himself. A sea lawyer like you ought to know the rules, George. First I get a chance to defend myself. Fair's fair. Right, Dick?"

"Well, I guess when you put it that way. Yeah, you oughta have a chance to defend yourself. Right, boys?"

Despite George's glowers, there was a reluctant chorus of "Yes."

"Okay. Let's hear the charges."

"You want charges?" George yelled. "I'll give you charges. Number one: you've made a complete foul-up of this cruise; you can't deny it. Two: we had the enemy trapped in this here bunker and you let them go. Why they wanted out, I don't know. But they did and you let 'em. Three, you wouldn't let us attack 'em once they was out. And four? Four is this here kid."

"That it?" Silver asked quietly.

"Enough to fry us all at Sing Sing."

"Okay, I'll answer all four, one by one. Number one: I fouled up this cruise, did I? You know damned well I told you how neat and clean I wanted it all done. But nooooooo: 'Let's have a drink, John. Can't we go ashore, John? Can't we kill 'em now, John?' Hurry, hurry, hurry. Well, here's where you hurried to. If you'da listened to me, you'd be lounging aboard the *Hispaniola* now, sitting down to a fine cooked supper to build up your strength to load more gold. So before you cast blame, thank the boys responsible: thank Anderson and Hands and you, George Merry! You're the last alive of that mob of screw-ups, so you figure that somehow gives you the right to stand for captain? Christ, chief undertaker is more your speed, George. 'Vote for me,' says George. Let me tell you, boys, you vote for George Merry and I'll guarantee you'll join your mates in a locker presided over by a certain Davy Jones."

Silver paused to let his words sink in, which, judging by the faces of George and his backers, they did. Deeply.

"That's for Number one," Silver growled, mopping sweat with his red handkerchief. He'd been yelling loudly. Now his tone grew quieter. "What I don't understand is how the women who called themselves your mothers ever allowed you to go to sea. I'd rather sail alone through a U-boat wolfpack than cross a millpond with you lubbers."

Morgan piped up, "What about the other charges, John?"

"Oh, the others. You say this cruise is fouled up? You don't know *how* fouled up. We're so close to the electric chair I got a tingling in the seat of my pants. Any of you guys ever seen Sing Sing from the North River? . . . Seamen steaming up to Albany, they'll say, 'Did you hear they're frying Long John Silver in there tonight? I knew him well. Used to be careful till he fell in with the wrong crowd. Watch close, you'll see the lights dim when they throw the switch. There he goes! Rest in peace, Long John. See you in hell . . .'

"That's how close we are to frying, boys, thanks to George and Hands and Anderson and some other fools. So if you want to know about charge four—that boy—that boy is our hostage. You want to kill our hostage? Our last chance?

"As for number three charge? Why didn't we kill 'em when they marched out of the bunker? Aside from the fact that they weren't about to make killing them easy, aren't you kind of glad to have a real live doctor to come visit daily? You, with your head busted. Or you, George Merry, you jerk, with that fever rattling your skeleton and your eyes the color of lemon peel? And maybe none of you heard that one of these days old Blandly is going to send out a search ship he can charge to the senator. Another reason we'll be glad of a hostage.

"Let me see, what else? Oh, yeah—charge two: why I made a bargain to let them leave this bunker. Disregarding for the moment the fact that you SOBs crawled on your knees begging me to take it because you happened to be starving—disregarding your initial gratitude for putting food in your bellies—here's why!"

And he threw down on the floor a piece of paper I immediately recognized—the yellowed chart, with the three red crosses that my mother and I had found in the bottom of Billy Bones's duffel bag.

Why Dr. Livesey had given it to Long John was a mystery to which I hadn't a clue. They leapt on it like a pack of cats on a crippled mouse, whooping, hollering, ripping it out of one another's hands. Cursing and giggling, they acted as if they had their hands on the gold itself and were sailing home happily with it.

"That's Flint!" roared one. "J.F."

"Terrific," said George Merry. "How the hell are we supposed to get it off the island with no ship?"

Silver jumped off his ammunition box and braced himself with one hand on the wall. "That's it, George. One more peep out of you and I'll tear your head off. How? Why don't you tell me how, smart guy—you and the rest that lost me my ship with your screwing around, damn you. No, you don't have the brains to tell me how. You can talk real slick, but you couldn't think your way out of a wet paper bag."

"He's right about that," said old Morgan.

"Right? Damn right. You lost the ship. I found the treasure. Who's the better man at finding gold? And now I resign, goddamnit. Elect who the hell you want to be captain now. I'm out of it."

"Silver!" they cried. "Long live Barbecue! Barbecue for captain!"

"Are you sure?" he asked silkily.

"Yeeeessssss!"

Silver picked up his crutch and clumped to the door. For a long while he gazed out at the night. "Okay. If that's the way you want it, fine by me. Oh, George, pal, looks like you're going to have to try again sometime—or get your own crew. Fortunately for you, I'm not a vengeful guy. I'm easygoing. Easygoing John. I know they call me that behind my back. As for these ballots—not much use now. You went and spoiled Dick's Bible for nothing."

Dick said, "It doesn't really hurt it, does it? You can still swear on it, right?"

"A Bible with the fly leaves torn out by dishonest men?— forget it!" He crumpled the ballots in his huge hand and tossed them to me. "Here you go, Jim. Souvenir of your first mutiny."

They toasted their renewed captain vows with rum and warm Coke and soon everyone went back to bed. Everyone but George Merry. Maybe Silver took revenge, maybe he didn't, but he made George stand night watch, with a warning he'd slit his throat if he fell asleep.

I lay awake for hours, my mind racing with the events of a long, violent day. I had awakened wave-tossed in my little kayak, and here I was back in the bunker as Silver's hostage.

In between I had killed a man who had tried to kill me. But the high point was seeing Silver in action, controlling his mutinous gang with one hand while pulling every trick in the book with the other to save his miserable life.

30

On Parole

"SICK CALL!" A clear, sweet voice awakened all of us, including George the sentry, who had fallen asleep in the doorway. "Rise and shine for sick call!"

Dr. Livesey. I jumped up in joy before I remembered how I'd sneaked off. I was ashamed to meet her eye and hung behind the others crowding toward the door.

Wherever she came from, she must have started out in the dark. The day was just breaking; where she waited, between the woods and the barbed wire fence, the night fog still gathered around her knees. She was wearing a khaki shirt and slacks and had wrapped mosquito netting around her hat like a veil.

"Good morning, Doc. Top of the morning to you," cried Silver. Wide awake and smiling broadly, he had apparently slept like a baby. "Bright and early. Early bird gets the worm—George, get off your duff and help the lady through the fence. All your patients are doing well, Doctor, everyone on the mend, stronger and meaner every day."

Happily he chattered on, standing atop the hill, with his crutch in one hand and the other braced on the bunker— cheery Barbecue the sea cook.

"Oh boy, do we have a surprise for you, Doc. New recruit joined up. Got ourselves a little visitor in the night.

Dropped by to say hello and we convinced him he'd sleep safer here with his old shipmates than out in the jungle."

Dr. Livesey by now had climbed through the fence and was close to Silver. I could hear a change in her voice as she asked, "Not Jim?"

"One and the same," crowed Silver. "Our dear old Jim."

The doctor stopped in her tracks. She didn't say a word, but it was a full minute before she seemed able to move on.

"Well, that's marvelous," she said at last. "But as you'd say, Silver, 'Work first, play later.' Sick call. Let's see your patients."

She swept into the bunker with a grim nod to me, threw back her veil, opened her black bag, and went to work on the sick. She seemed perfectly at ease, though she must have known that trapped in there with Silver's gang she was inches from death at every second. But she acted as warm and friendly as if she were making a house call back on Long Island. Her easy manner seemed to thrust them into a gentler role, as if they were still honest hands sailing the *Hispaniola* and she was the ship's doctor.

"You're doing well, my friend," she said to a man who two days ago had attempted to scale the wire to kill us all. "Close call, mister. You have a head like a cannonball. How about you, George—oh boy, look at your temperature. No wonder your eyes are yellow as a school bus. Did you take your medicine? Did he, men?"

"Tried to spit it out," answered Morgan. "We made him swallow."

"Excellent," said Dr. Livesey in her pleasantest way. "Seeing as how I'm your doctor—or prison doctor, you might say—I'm professionally bound to save your skins for the electric chair."

The gang exchanged murderous glances, but took her jibe in silence.

"Dick don't feel so hot," said one.

"Let me see your tongue, Dick. Holy smoke, your tongue

would scare a snapping turtle. You picked up another fever."

"No surprise there," said Morgan. "That's what you get for abusing your Bible."

"No," retorted the doctor. "That's what you all get for sleeping by a swamp. Bunch of horses' asses, don't even know to camp on high ground? You'll have malaria in your systems for the rest of your lives. Silver, you surprise me. I'd have thought you at least would know something about simple hygiene."

She gave them all medicine, which they swallowed down more like school kids than killers. "Okay, that's it for today. Try to get plenty of rest and try to go easy on the booze. Oh, by the way, I'd like a moment with the kid."

She nodded casually in my direction.

George Merry was still gagging his medicine. But when he heard the doctor ask to see me, he leapt to block the door, loudly cursing, "No!"

"*Si-lence!*" roared Silver, and glowered like a lion. "Doc," he went on, in his quieter, friendlier tone, "I figured you'd want to have a chat with Jim, seeing as you always liked the boy and looked after him. And of course we're all grateful for you treating our sick and wounded. Hell, we're drinking down your medicine like rum and Coke. So I think I've come up with a way we can take a chance on letting you talk to Jim. Jim, will you give me your word you won't try to escape?"

I nodded, glad to agree to anything for a moment alone with Dr. Livesey.

"Scout's honor and cross your heart and hope to die?"

"I promise, John."

"Okay, Doc. You step outside the wire and I'll bring the boy down and you two can have your talk through the wire. Thanks again for coming, Doc. Take care and please give our best to the senator and Captain Smollett."

The gang exploded the second the doctor was out the

door. John had kept them in check with black looks, but now the bunker rocked with a chorus of angry disapproval. They accused Silver of a double-cross—of trying to cut a separate deal for himself, of selling them out for his freedom. In a word, they accused him of doing exactly what he *was* doing. That seemed so obvious that I couldn't imagine how he could convincingly deny it. But he was twice the man they were and held a powerful mandate from his re-election the night before. He called them fools and asses and every kind of idiot, claimed it was vital I talk to the doctor, and fluttered the chart in their faces.

"You want to break the treaty the same day we go hunting gold?" he roared contemptuously. "Not on your scummy lives. We're on my timetable now. We'll break the treaty when I say we're ready to break the treaty. I'm calling the shots and until we break the treaty we'll accommodate her any way she wants—no buts, George. If she asks to conduct medical experiments on your liver, we'll send it in a jar."

Ordering them to light the breakfast fire, he stalked out into the sunlight, one hand on his crutch, the other on my shoulder.

"Not too fast, kid," he whispered. "They'll cut us down if they think we're running for it. Nice and easy now. Just don't make 'em think we're in a rush."

Backs tingling with the strong probability of rifles tracking us, we strolled slowly down the stump-littered slope to where Dr. Livesey waited on the other side of the wire fence. When we were close enough to speak, Silver stopped and planted his crutch.

"I hope you remember this, Doc. Jim'll tell you how I saved his bacon last night, even though it meant they voted me out of the captaincy—don't worry, I got reelected. But it's a mighty thin line I'm walking. So I'm hoping you'll maybe be able to put in a good word for me. Keeping in mind it's not only my skin I'm trying to save, but Jim's too.

Doc, I'm asking you to give me a little bit of hope, something I can cling to. Please."

Silver had changed completely now that we were away from the bunker. His cheeks had caved in. His voice trembled. At last, I thought, he's speaking straight from the heart.

"John, are you afraid?" asked Dr. Livesey.

"Doc, I've never been a coward. And if I was I wouldn't admit it. No, what's shaking me up is thinking about the electric chair. I don't want to fry, Doc. So I'm asking you not to forget the good I done—along with the bad, of course—like how I'm letting you talk alone with Jim. You'll remember, right?"

Crutch sinking deep in the sand, he limped back out of earshot and sat down on a stump, whistling "The Monkeys." From there, by swiveling his head, he could watch both me and Dr. Livesey and the gang emerging from the bunker to build a fire and cook breakfast.

"Jim, Jim, Jim," said the doctor sadly. "You've really stepped in it this time . . . Jeez, I love you too much to blame you, but I do have to say this: before Captain Smollett was wounded you wouldn't have dared run away. You waited till the poor man was flat on his back; then you deserted. That wasn't very nice."

That was all I had to hear. I burst into tears. "Please don't say that. I've blamed myself over and over already and now they're going to kill me—they would have already if Silver hadn't stopped them. I probably deserve to die, but he says they'll torture me first and I'm really afraid."

"Jim," she interrupted sharply. "I can't allow this. Hop through the fence. We'll try to run for it. Here, I'll lift this strand, you—"

"No."

"Why not?"

"I gave my word. I promised."

"Oh, for crissake, hop through the fence. You're just a boy."

"No," I said, knowing in that second that I was no longer just a boy. "You wouldn't go back on your word. Neither would the senator. Neither would Captain Smollett. I gave my word and Silver trusted me."

"Jim—" she started sternly.

"Wait. You didn't let me finish. The reason I'm afraid of torture is I'd give away where the ship is."

"The ship?"

"She's beached in North Inlet. You can winch her off at high tide." Quickly, I filled her in on my sailing adventure with Israel Hands and company. When I was done, Dr. Livesey gazed reflectively up at the bunker, over at Silver, then back to me.

"Funny pattern developing here. Every time, one way or another you manage to save our lives. I think it's up to us to save yours. You overheard the plot. You found Ben Gunn— the best thing you'll do if you live to ninety. Jeez, speaking of Ben Gunn—Hey, Silver! Silver," she called. "Let me give you a piece of advice."

Silver limped our way.

"Don't go rushing off after the treasure."

"Fine by me," said Silver. "But the only thing keeping that crowd up there from slitting my and Jim's throats is the promise of me leading them to the gold."

"In that case, here's another piece of advice. When you find it, get ready to duck."

"You're confusing me, Doc. What you're up to, why you left the bunker, why you gave me the chart, I haven't the foggiest idea. But I did what you asked, without any encouragement from you. But now you're talking crazy. If you won't tell me what you're talking about, I'm throwing in the towel."

"Sorry," said the doctor. "I can't say any more. It's not

my secret to share. But I'll take a chance—hoping Smollett doesn't ream me out for it—by promising that if we both get out of this mess alive, I'll speak up for you—truth only—to save your miserable skin."

Silver glowed with triumph. "Thank you, Doctor. Thank you from the bottom of my heart. You couldn't have been kinder if you were my own mother."

Dr. Livesey shuddered. "That's my offer. Now here's some more advice: keep Jim close to you and yell your head off when you need help. Goodbye, Jim."

She leaned through the wire and kissed my cheek, then bounded into the woods.

31

The Treasure Hunt—Flint's Arrow

J IM," SAID SILVER. "You saved my life. I saw the doc-sie try to get you to run. And I saw you say no. Thanks, kid. I won't forget. It's the first good break I've had since we had our heads handed to us in the attack. Maybe things are looking up—Now look, we've got to go hunt the gold. The doc-sie's issued us some kind of sealed orders. I don't like not knowing what's up, but we got no choice. So stick close—back to back—and maybe we'll save our necks."

"Come and get it," came a yell from the cooks, and soon we were hunched over plates of fried bacon. They had lit a fire big enough to roast an ox. It was so hot you could only approach from upwind and even then you had to shield your face. Needless to say, the bacon was sort of crispy. And they'd cooked three times as much as we needed. Laughing like a hyena, one of them chucked the leftovers into the flames, which roared higher on the fat.

This was the hand-to-mouth attitude Silver had always complained about. Wasted firewood, wasted food, sleeping sentries. They were plenty mean and dangerous in a short fight, but totally incapable of the long haul. On the other hand, those who had survived this long were proof of the power of sudden viciousness.

This morning, Silver ignored their behavior. Gobbling up

bacon, tossing scraps to Captain Flint nattering on his shoulder, his only comment was "Lucky you got Barbecue thinking for you, boys. I found out what I wanted. They got the ship hidden somewhere. Seeing as we're the ones with the boats, we got a good chance of finding it after we get the gold. And I think even the most lunkheaded of you will agree that with gold and ship, we'll be winners."

He went on like that as they ate, laughing and chuckling, building their courage and, I suspected, his own too. I also began to suspect that he was still choosing sides.

"As far as our hostage is concerned," he continued, "he's had his last talk with his pals. Thanks to him, I figured out they got the ship."

"Doc tell you that?"

"Not in so many words. Anyway, they've had their last chat and from now on the kid stays closer to me than fleas. Just in case we need him. After we get the gold, and we're sailing away from here, we'll let Jim have a share of what he deserves—for all his kindness."

His men were certainly happy again, but I was feeling lower and lower. Silver was at least twice a traitor. What was to stop him from jumping ship a third time if his latest scheme worked out? His men *were* seamen. If he found the gold and they started motoring around the island they'd find the ship in half a day. And when it came down to a choice between a bare escape from the electric chair or gold and freedom, my pal Long John would toss me overboard without a moment's hesitation.

But even if he kept his deal with Dr. Livesey, I was still in danger. Because once his gang realized we were pulling a fast one, we'd have to fight for our lives—Long John on only one leg and me a boy—against five strong seamen.

And if that weren't enough to worry me, what were my own friends up to? Why had they abandoned the safety of the bunker? Why had they given Silver the chart? And what in the name of God had the doctor meant when she warned

Silver to "duck" when we found the gold? Needless to say, breakfast went down like a cold cement block.

We made quite a picture as we started out to hunt the gold—all in filthy, muddy clothes, all but me armed to the teeth. Silver had two shotguns, one slung over his back, the other across his chest. A machete hung from his belt. Pistol butts stuck out of his pockets. And if this walking arsenal didn't look strange enough, Captain Flint rode his shoulder, cracking seeds stored in Silver's hat and screaming, "Pieces of eight! Pieces of eight!"

Silver tied a rope around my waist. He held the other end, sometimes in his hand, sometimes in his teeth, dragging me along, so that I was never farther than three feet from him, like a dog on a leash.

The rest of the gang carried picks and shovels—the first tools they'd taken ashore from the *Hispaniola*—and canned food and crackers and cookies, and rum, of course, all of which they had found in the bunker. Silver had told the truth about his bargain with Dr. Livesey. If he hadn't traded for food, they'd be drinking swamp water and trying to shoot birds for dinner, Ben Gunn having frightened the goats into the hills.

So armed and loaded down we started out—even the guy with the head wound, who should have stayed in the shade—down to the beach where they'd left the launches. They'd screwed up the boats. They'd got water in the gas in one and, falling-down drunk, had smashed the seats in the other. We bailed that one out, got the engine started and headed into the harbor, towing the second, with two guys in it bailing frantically.

In Silver's boat, they discussed the chart. The red cross was too big to be more than a general guide, of course. And Flint's notes were somewhat ambiguous. They read, you may recall:

Tall tree, Spyglass shoulder, bearing a point to the N of NNE.
Skeleton Island ESE and by E.
Ten feet.

We were looking for a tall tree. Dead ahead of the boats a plateau rose two or three hundred feet above the anchorage. To the north it joined the southern shoulder of Spyglass Hill. To the south it rose to the rough cliffs of Mizzenmast Hill. On top, the plateau was covered with pine trees of various heights. Here and there one thrust up forty or fifty feet higher than the others. Which one was Captain Flint's "tall tree" could only be ascertained from the spot determined by the compass readings.

That didn't stop Silver's crew. Before we were halfway across the harbor, everyone was voting loudly for his favorite tree.

"Wait till we're there," Silver cautioned.

We finally made it across and beached the boats at the mouth of the second river, which runs down a wooded ravine of Spyglass Hill. Bearing left, we started up the slope to the plateau.

At first, thick mud and dense marsh grass made it slow climbing. But little by little, as the hill got steeper, the ground firmed up underfoot and the woods thinned out until we were in a really pretty part of the island. Sweet-smelling broom and flowering shrubs replaced the grass. In among the pine trees the air turned fresher still and sunbeams danced among the tall trunks.

My captors danced too, fanning out and forging ahead, shouting happily. Silver and I plodded after them, Long John struggling on his crutch and jerking the rope around my waist. Sometimes when the ground got rough, I had to help him or he would have fallen backward down the hill.

We had struggled on like this about a half mile, and were nearing the rim of the plateau, when the man on the left started yelling. He sounded terrified, screaming fearfully as the others ran to help him.

"He couldn'ta found the gold," panted old Morgan, racing past us from the right. "It's on top."

When Silver and I finally caught up, what we found sure wasn't gold. Stretched out at the base of a big pine tree, all entwined in vines and creepers, which had started detaching some of the smaller bones, was a human skeleton.

I shivered. Shreds of rotten cloth lay among the bones.

"A seaman," said George Merry, examining the rags. "At least this was a good pea jacket, once."

"I don't think we'd find a preacher here," said Silver. "But why are his bones laying that way? That's not natural."

John was right. On second glance, when we got over the shock, we saw that the body lay in a strange position. Except where the smaller bones had been messed up by birds scavenging his flesh and the creepers wrapping them, the dead man lay in an unnaturally straight line. His feet pointed one way; his arms, stretched overhead like he was diving off a highboard, pointed exactly opposite, straight as clock hands at six o'clock.

"I got a funny idea," said Silver. "Here's the compass. There's the highest peak of Skeleton Island sticking up like a tooth. Take a bearing along the bones."

I took the bearing, as he'd taught me. The body pointed straight at Skeleton Island. The compass read ESE by E.

"Thought so!" crowed Silver. "He's pointing right at the gold. Jeez, if Flint weren't a ghoulish bastard. It's one of *his* jokes, you can bet on it. Dragged this poor slob up here and spread him with a compass. Flint was warped."

Silver leaned over his crutch, jerking me closer to the bones than I wanted to be, and grabbed the skull, which seemed to be nested in straw. "Blond hair. You know who this is? This is Allardyce. Tom, you remember Allardyce, don't you?"

"Son of a bitch owed me money," said Morgan. "Borrowed my knife too, never gave it back."

"Speaking of knives," someone said. "Where's his knife? Flint wouldn't pick a dead man's pocket."

George Merry felt among the bones. "Weird. No knife, no buttons. Not even the zipper from his fly."

"Weird," Silver agreed. "Jesus, mates, we'd be in trouble if Flint were still alive. He killed six. We're six. He'd do us too."

"Flint's dead as a doornail," said Morgan. "I saw the body with my own eyes. Billy took me in and showed me."

"Dead and in hell," said the guy with the banged-up head. "But if there was ever a ghost that came back it'll be him. Nobody ever died as bad as Flint—Cursing God and screaming for rum and Coke. They brought him a priest. It was hot and they had the window open. You could hear Flint singing "The Monkey Tails" in the priest's face. The man was dying and he knew it but he kept singing. I can't stand that damned song anymore."

"Pipe down," growled Silver. "Flint's dead and gone, and he damned sure don't walk. Let's get the gold."

We started up again, but no one was jumping and shouting anymore, despite the lovely weather. The men walked side by side, bunched close, whispering about the skeleton.

32

The Treasure Hunt—
The Voice in the Trees

W E REACHED THE rim of the plateau and sat down to rest the sick and wounded. As the ground tilted a bit to the west, we could see far and wide. Over the treetops gleamed the Point of Woods, white-fringed with surf, while in back of us we looked down on Captain Kidd's anchorage and Skeleton Island, and, clear across the barrier beach, the eastern lowlands and the open sea. Straight above us rose Spyglass Hill, speckled with green pines and black precipices. Breakers muttered in the distance; nearby, insects chirped in the brush. But we were totally alone. Not a man ashore, not a ship at sea, so that the view seemed to resonate with solitude.

While he rested, Silver took more bearings with his compass. "I see three separate 'tall trees,' on about the right line with Skeleton Island. 'Spyglass shoulder' must be that point there. Piece of cake to find the gold now. Maybe we ought to eat lunch first."

"I kind of lost my appetite," said Morgan. "Flint and his goddamned skeleton jokes."

"Well, pal, you just thank your lucky stars he's dead."

"God, Flint was ugly," whispered another. "All blue in the face."

"That was the booze made him blue," said George Merry. "Fact of life. Or death."

They had lost their voices since they found the skeleton, talking quieter and quieter of death and ghosts and terrible Flint. I could hear the soft sounds of the woods, despite their constant talking. Then all of a sudden, from the trees nearby, a thin, high trembling voice began to sing.

"Oh, the monkeys have no tails in Zamboanga . . ."

Six faces went white as milk. Half the gang leapt to their feet, clutching each other. Morgan cringed on the ground.

"It's Flint!" cried Merry. "Oh God, oh God."

"They were chewed off by the—"

The song stopped suddenly, breaking off right in the middle of a note, as if someone had clapped a hand over the singer's mouth, or strangled him. Having risen from the trees on such a clear sunny day, it sounded kind of pleasant to me. But not to my captors.

"No, no, no," stammered Silver, white as the others, but struggling to make sense of it. "It's a trick. It's a trick. I don't know the voice, but it's some son of a bitch screwing around, alive as you and me."

He gained more courage as he spoke and some color returned to his face. The others heard it in his voice and began to get ahold of themselves too, when from the distance we heard the voice again. Not a song this time, but a command that echoed among the cliffs of Spyglass Hill.

"Darby M'Graw," it wailed like an old-time steam whistle. "Darby M'Graw. Darby M'Graw!" again and again and again. Then, higher and shrieking a filthy curse, "Bring the booze, Darby."

Silver's gang froze, eyes popping. For a long minute after the voice died away, they just stared in silent terror.

"Christ on a crutch," moaned Morgan. "Those was Flint's last words. Last thing he said before he died. Heard him with my own ears: 'Bring the booze, Darby.' "

Dick whipped out his Bible and started praying.

Only Silver remained unbroken. He was shivering so hard

I could hear his teeth rattling in his head, but he didn't give up.

"No one on this whole damned island ever heard of Darby. No one but us six." He took a deep breath into his lungs and seemed to gather his body by an effort of will and spirit.

"Now hear this, you guys. I'm here for the gold and no one is stopping me—man or devil. I was never scared of Flint alive and goddamn I'll face him down dead too. We got five million bucks of gold a quarter mile from here. And I never met a salvage man yet who'd give up five million bucks to an old rummy with a blue mug—alive *or* dead!"

"Easy, John," Merry cautioned. "Don't piss 'im off."

I was amazed by how superstitious they were. On the other hand, if I had killed as many men as they had over the years, maybe the dead would frighten me too.

But even while the others huddled in fear, Silver was getting over his scare. "Piss who off?" he demanded. "Didn't you pantywaists hear the echo? If ghosts don't cast a shadow, they sure as hell don't echo either."

While I personally did not believe in ghosts, Silver's echo theory seemed a pretty weak argument against them. His men, however, embraced it heartily.

Even his enemy George Merry applauded. "Good thinking, John. Full speed astern, boys, we're steaming in the wrong direction. And now that I think about it, it sounded sort of like Flint's voice, but not exactly, you know? It was more like somebody else—like—"

"Ben Gunn!" roared Silver.

"You're right. You're right!" cried Morgan, raising his belly from the ground. "That's Ben Gunn, all right."

"What's so great about that?" asked Dick. "Ben Gunn's dead too."

The old salvors laughed.

"Nobody's afraid of that sadsack," said Merry. "Dead or alive, Ben Gunn's harmless."

Instantly, white faces grew bright with color and suddenly all was right in their world. I realized they didn't fear ghosts as much as they feared Flint. I couldn't help but recall what Silver had said when I listened from the barrel: they were afraid of Flint, but Flint was afraid of him.

They listened a little while longer, and when there was no repeat of the singing or wailing, they picked up their tools and started out jauntily after Merry, who walked with Silver's compass to keep in line with Skeleton Island. Merry had said the truth: dead or alive, nobody feared Ben Gunn.

Dick, however, still clung to his Bible and shot frightened looks at every shadow. Silver teased him. "I already told you, Dick, you ruined your Bible. It couldn't stop a ghost any bigger than your pinky. Hey, relax, pal. Nothing to worry about."

But Dick could not relax. Nor was it only ghosts that troubled him. He was getting sicker and sicker, as Dr. Livesey had predicted he would. Exhausted by the heat and the climb, he burned with a fever that reddened his cheeks and turned his eyes wild.

It was actually easy walking along the summit, for our route followed a gentle slope to the west. And it was fairly open, with the pines standing apart from one another. Between clumps of azalea and nutmeg, broad open spaces baked in the sun. Heading as we did nearly northwest across the island, we drew closer and closer to Spyglass Hill, while to our other side stretched ever larger views of the western bay where I had drifted in Ben's kayak.

We reached the first of the tall trees. But the compass bearing indicated it was not the one. The second, too, proved wrong. The third was a giant, rising two hundred feet, with a red trunk as big as a house, and a crown that could have shaded a baseball diamond. From the sea it must have stood out like a lighthouse.

My friends broke into a run, and if dead Flint and every dead man in his crew had leapt up now, Silver's men would have trampled them into the ground. Life loomed before them—riches and pleasures—a few short yards ahead—booze, women, Cadillacs, and fancy hotels.

Silver pounded after them on his crutch. His nostrils flared; he cursed at the bugs landing on his sweating face and jerked furiously at the rope around my waist, urging me on with deadly looks. This close to five million dollars in gold, he didn't bother to pretend, and I knew exactly what he was thinking. All bets were off—if he even remembered his promises or the doctor's warnings. It was suddenly so simple again. All he had to do was dig up the gold, find the ship, board her at night, cut every throat on the island, and sail away in splendor—exactly as he had intended from the very beginning.

Scared silly, I stumbled as I struggled to keep up. Silver jerked the rope and threw me another murderous look. Dick had fallen back, shambling behind us, babbling feverish prayers and curses. It's going to happen again, I realized with a sinking heart. This peaceful glade we were entering would ring again with death as it had when the blue-faced, monstrous Captain Flint slaughtered the six who had buried his gold.

"Gung-ho!" shouted Merry; and the others, roaring and laughing like madmen, yelled "Banzai!" and charged after him.

Suddenly, just ten yards ahead of Silver and me, they skidded to a confused stop. We heard a low cry. Silver hobbled faster, driving hard on his crutch. Then he and I also skidded to a stop. At our feet was a huge hole. It wasn't a very new hole. The sides had caved in and grass had sprouted on the bottom, and a vine or two twined merrily around a broken pickax and some smashed crates. One of the crates was branded with the name *Walrus*. Flint's ship.

Someone had beat us to it.

33

The Fall of a Chieftain

NO HOLE IN the history of the world ever looked so empty.

All six stood stunned as if each had been hit in the face with a brick. Silver recovered first. No one knew better than I how he'd pounded along with every fiber of his being, aiming for that gold. I had felt him shaking through the rope. Suddenly, in one second, he had lost. But he alone was able to swallow loss and think fast before the others even had time to digest the immensity of their disappointment.

"Jim," he whispered. "Take this and stand by."

And he slipped me a .38.

At the same time, he led me quietly northward. With a couple of steps we'd put the hole between us and them. He gave me a look and a kind of half wink as if to say, We're in a tight one now, pal.

I couldn't have agreed more. And if I could have had one wish granted at that moment, I would have been on the far side of the island. Still, when he winked, I could not resist whispering, "Now whose side are you on?"

His angry men gave him no chance to answer. Cursing and howling, they leapt into the hole, threw the broken crates out, and dug with their fingers. Morgan found a chip of gold that looked like it had broken off an ingot. He held it up, cursing. They passed it around. "Gotta be worth a hundred bucks," said Morgan.

"Hundred bucks," roared George Merry, shaking it at Long John. "This is your five million, you son of a bitch? You never fouled things up? All our fault, eh? You two-bit son of a—"

"Dig away, boys," Silver smiled. "You'll hit potatoes soon."

"Potatoes!" screamed Merry. "You guys hear him? He knew it all along. Look at his face—he knew!"

Silver laughed. "Standing for captain again, George? You certainly are an ambitious guy."

But this time they were all on Merry's side. One by one they climbed out of the hole, firing furious looks our way. About all Silver and I had going for us was that they climbed out the other side of the hole, so again we had it between us.

There we stood, like a pack of dogs on one side and a pair of worried cats on the other. Five of them. Two of us, a cripple and a boy. Silver stood still as stone, straight as his crutch, and watched them. He was cool. And he was brave. No question he was brave.

George Merry seemed to think his men needed a pep talk.

"Count 'em, boys. Two of 'em, alone. The raggedy-assed cripple that suckered us in, and that miserable midget whose heart I'm going to roast on a stick. Count of three, we take 'em. One . . . two . . ."

He was raising his arm for three, when shots rang out from the nutmeg trees. Crack! Crack! Crack! George Merry fell headfirst in the hole. The guy with the head bandage spun in a full circle and collapsed on his side, dead but still twitching. The other three whirled and ran for it.

Long John pulled two pistols and emptied them into the struggling Merry, whose eyes rolled up at him in sightless agony. "George," said Silver, "we're even."

Dr. Livesey, Gray, and Ben Gunn came charging out of

the nutmeg trees training weapons on the escaping men. "After 'em!" cried the doctor. "Head 'em off. Don't let 'em get the boats."

We ran through the bushes, with Silver struggling along behind us. Bound to his crutch, he worked like ten men to keep up. Later the doctor told me it was almost impossible to imagine the punishment he forced on his body. But he was still thirty yards behind us when we reached the rim of the plateau.

"Relax! There they are running the wrong way. No hurry."

He was right. They were heading straight for Mizzenmast Hill. We were already between them and the boats. So we sat down to catch our breath while Long John, wiping his face, slowly caught up.

"Thanks, Doc. Nick of time for me and Jim . . . So it *is* you, Ben Gunn," he added. "You're something else."

"I'm Ben Gunn, all right," my goat-skinned friend replied, scuffing the ground in embarrassment. "How you doing, Mr. Silver? I'm doing fine, says you."

"Ben, Ben," murmured Silver. "I can't believe you're the one who did me in."

Dr. Livesey asked Gray to retrieve one of the pickaxes the fleeing gang had dropped. Then, as we headed down the hill, she gave us a brief rundown of what had happened. Needless to say, she had Silver's full attention. Not to mention his astonishment that poor dumb Ben Gunn, the fool, was the hero of her story.

He'd found the skeleton while on one of his lonely walks around the island, a fact I should have guessed by the missing knife and buttons. He had found the treasure. He had dug it up. He had carried it—load after heavy load of ingots on his back—from the giant pine tree all the way across the island to Twin Peaks Hill, where he hid it in a cave. He had staggered off with his last load two months before the *Hispaniola* dropped anchor in Captain Kidd's harbor.

Dr. Livesey had coaxed the secret out of him the afternoon of the attack. Then, when she woke up the next morning and saw the ship had gone, she went off into the woods, found Silver, and gave him the chart, knowing it now led only to a hole in the ground. She traded our food, too—knowing Ben's cave was full of smoked goat meat—and the bunker and everything in it for the chance to get her wounded patient away from the swamp malaria and up to the high ground of Twin Peaks Hill to guard the gold.

"I hated leaving you, Jim," she told me. "But I didn't know where you'd run to."

But this morning, when she realized that I'd be the enraged gang's prisoner the moment they found the treasure missing, she had raced back to the cave, left Senator Trelawney to protect Captain Smollett, and cut back across the island with Abe Gray and Ben Gunn. But we had had too big a head start on them, so Ben, who was fast as a goat, galloped ahead. It was six against one, but he got a brainstorm to scare them with his ghost act, which slowed them up enough to let the doctor and Gray set up their ambush.

"Lucky for me I had Jim along," interrupted Silver. "Without him, you'd have let them shoot me down like a dog."

"A dirty dog," Dr. Livesey agreed cheerfully.

By the end of her story, we had reached the boat. She handed Gray the pickax and told him to break up the boat we had towed. Then we all climbed into the other and headed out to sea.

It was a run of eight or nine miles to North Inlet. The outboard started acting up, but Silver got it going again and we made good time on the smooth sea. Dr. Livesey and I exchanged a glance as we rounded the southeast corner of the island, both of us thinking that, impossible as it seemed, we had towed the *Hispaniola* around this same point only four days ago.

As we motored past Twin Peaks Hill we could see the

dark opening to Ben Gunn's cave, and standing in front of it, waving happily, the senator.

"Top o' the morning!" bellowed Silver.

Another three miles and we slipped into the narrow mouth of North Inlet, and what did we find there but the *Hispaniola* merrily adrift. The moon-pulled high tide had floated her off the beach, so all we had to do was climb aboard and drop her spare anchor in deep water. We left Gray to guard her, and took the boat into Rum Cove, the nearest point to Ben Gunn's treasure cave.

A gentle hill rose from the beach to the cave. The senator met us on top. He pounded me on the back, chortling that next time he needed a ship stolen he'd turn to me. He threw his other big arm around Dr. Livesey and gave her a hug, laughing happily, until Silver tried to shake his hand.

"Silver, you thieving, lowdown, lying, murdering bastard. The doc says you two cut a deal and I'm supposed to testify in your favor. I'll go along. But you know and I know you've got seventeen dead men on your conscience."

"Thank you kindly, Senator."

The senator turned purple. "Thank me again and I'll shove that crutch down your throat. Sideways."

We went into the cave. It was big and airy inside with a spring-fed pool. Captain Smollett lay beside a fire. And in the corner, burnished by the flickering flames, was a huge stack of gold bars. I went over and touched one, stroked its cold, smooth surface. Each was stamped with a swastika and the date 1945.

This was Flint's treasure, which had killed most of the men who had sailed on the *Hispaniola*. Killed the six men who had helped Flint bury it. Killed the honest salvage divers whose airhoses Flint's renegades had cut. Killed the crew of the U-boat that had smuggled it across the Atlantic. Killed the thousands, millions, whose coins and watches and necklaces and earrings had been melted into those cold, smooth ingots. How many had died, no one could know.

And yet, still on the island, were three who'd committed their full share of the crimes—Silver, old Morgan, and Ben Gunn.

"Jim," called the captain in a weak voice. "Come here, boy . . . Well, you did pretty well for yourself, though I doubt I'd go to sea with you again—you're too much of the lone wolf for a captain's taste." (I sort of liked the sound of that, and as the years have gone by, I've several times had to admit that the captain had my number.) "Who's that, there? Silver?"

"Silver, reporting, sir," said Long John, hobbling closer to throw a salute.

"Is that a fact?" was all the captain said.

What a victory feast I shared that night, surrounded by my friends. We gobbled down Ben Gunn's smoked goat, huge cans of Chef Boy-Ar-Dee ravioli from the ship, and Fig Newtons. For dessert, I contributed my stash of Mounds Bars, hidden so well on the *Hispaniola* that the mutineers never found it.

I knew then, and I know even better now, that no group of people were ever happier than we that night on Treasure Island. Silver sat at the edge of the firelight, scarfing down goat and ravioli, quick to jump to bring someone seconds, even chuckling along with our laughter—the same pleasant sea cook of the voyage out.

34

And Last

THE NEXT MORNING we got busy moving the gold. It was a mile by land to the beach, then three miles by boat to the ship, a huge job for so few people. We were too busy to worry much about the three still wandering the island. One lookout on the hill could protect us from ambush, and besides, it was pretty clear they'd had enough fighting, particularly with their only possible leader, George Merry, dead in an empty hole.

So the transfer went fast. Gray and Ben Gunn ran the boat, while the rest of us piled gold on the beach. The grown men could carry eight to twelve ingots at a time, tied up and slung over their shoulders by a rope. Dr. Livesey alternated six and eight. Four was my limit at first, then five as I built muscle—aching muscle. This went on for several days, each day seeing the pile get smaller and smaller. All this time we heard not a peep from the men who had escaped.

Then on the third night Dr. Livesey and I were taking a breather on the rim of the hill that overlooked the island's lowlands when we heard singing in the dark below.

"There they are," said the doctor.

"Drunk as skunks," Silver called behind us.

The cook, whom we allowed to hobble around loose,

seemed to think he was one of us again, despite a steady flow of nasty remarks aimed his way. Nothing we said bothered him and he remained as polite and docile as a collie. Only Ben Gunn was nice to him, being still afraid of his old chief petty officer. And I, of course, who owed him my life—though I had to wonder how things would have gone for me if Silver had found the gold.

Dr. Livesey answered him roughly. "Drunk or out of their minds with fever."

"Couldn't have said it better myself, Doc. Booze, fever, what do we care?"

She rounded on him, sneering, "I know you don't care. But if I knew it was fever, I'd have to go help them."

"Not a wise move in the dark, Doc. We wouldn't find much more than your pretty little carcass in the morning. I'm on your side, Doc, and I owe you a few, so let me tell you, you can't trust them."

"Takes one to know one," said the doctor, clearly troubled.

The next day we heard a gunshot in the distance and figured they were hunting for game to eat. We held a meeting and decided we had to leave them on the island—a decision that thrilled Ben Gunn and delighted Abe Gray. We left them some guns to hunt with and most of the smoked goat and canned goods and medicine, some scraps of clothing, some tools. To this stash on the beach, covered with a canvas, Dr. Livesey added a carton of Gauloises. And with that we motored out to the *Hispaniola*, shipped the launch, weighed anchor, and steamed out of North Inlet, flying Captain Smollett's last American flag.

The three escapees, who must have been watching more closely than we thought, burst out of the woods at the southern narrows, where the channel practically brushed the shore. They threw down their weapons, knelt on the sand, and raised their hands high, pleading for us to take them.

"Can't risk another mutiny," said Smollett from the hammock we'd rigged for him behind the helm. "Those three and our friendly cook make four."

Dr. Livesey ran out on deck, calling to them about the food and gear we'd left on the beach.

"Doc," they pleaded. "Save us. You're a good woman, save us." But when they saw the ship wasn't stopping, one of them snatched up his rifle and fired a shot that passed right over Silver's head. We ducked down behind the bulwarks and stayed down until we were out of the inlet and climbing the Atlantic swell.

By noon, when the peak of Spyglass Hill vanished astern and with it the last of Treasure Island, I felt only joy.

We were so shorthanded that we set a course for the nearest United States port, which turned out to be St. Thomas, Virgin Islands. It was a long haul anyway, and we got beat up a few times by squalls and gales. When we finally dropped anchor in a landlocked harbor, we were exhausted.

Smiling tourists gaped at our battered ship from the decks of cruise liners and bungalows on the shore. The sight of so many good-humored faces did a lot to banish memories of the dark and bloody island we had left behind. Dr. Livesey and Senator Trelawney took me ashore to call on the American governor, who fell all over himself to welcome the war-hero senator. We bought clean clothes and went to a wonderful restaurant and didn't get back to the ship until dawn.

Ben Gunn was waiting alone on deck, nervous and confused. What started as an explanation quickly became a confession. Silver had escaped.

Ben had helped him, assuring a livid Senator Trelawney that he had only done it to protect our lives. "If the man with one leg had stayed aboard, he'd have killed us all. Cut our throats in our sleep."

"I was hoping he'd try," growled the senator. "Well, that's that. At least he didn't take anything."

Ben Gunn commenced a nervous dance about the deck. "Well, sir, actually, he . . . took some gold. How much gold? you ask. Just a little, I say. Exactly how much? you demand. Just about five thousand dollars worth."

Silver had cut through a bulkhead—had probably been sawing at it throughout the whole voyage—and carted off four or five ingots with the unwitting help of a water-skiing tourist who gave him a ride ashore in one of the hotel speed-boats.

"Cheap at twice the price," said Dr. Livesey. "Main thing is he's gone."

We hired some hands and set north for New York, which we made two days before school started.

Mr. Blandly had already decided to send a search party, a fact he proved by presenting bills for a second ship, crew's wages, and bunker fuel.

Of all who had sailed on the *Hispaniola* only five came back. We hadn't lost as many as the *Titanic*, but our percentage, Dr. Livesey observed, was a lot worse. There was plenty of gold and few to share. And our shares affected our lives in about the way those who knew us could have predicted.

Captain Smollett has retired from the sea and gardens happily on the North Shore of Long Island. His occasional visits to Dr. Livesey usually prompt Senator Trelawney to break up some furniture.

Abe Gray studied for his master's ticket, got married, and bought a little coastal tanker he runs up and down the Great South Bay.

Poor Ben Gunn bought a Cadillac, drove to Las Vegas, and came home on a bus. The senator gave him a job mowing the lawns on his estate. The kids make fun of Ben, but he sings like a saint in the Bayport Methodist Choir.

We never heard of Silver again. I always thought he met up with his wife in California. I like to picture him hobbling around orange groves with Captain Flint clinging to his shoulder. At least I hope that's what happened, because if there is such a thing as an afterlife, his long-term future is pretty bleak.

Ben Gunn says that the jewels and silver that came off the U-boat are still buried where Flint hid them. As far as I'm concerned they can stay there, though Ben swears he knows where to look. Wild horses and the most powerful tugboats in the world couldn't drag me back to Treasure Island. I still have nightmares in which I hear the surf pounding like the hearts of everyone who died. Suddenly I'm awake—or hope I'm awake—with the voice of Captain Flint shrieking in my ears: "Pieces of eight! Pieces of eight! Pieces of eight!"

AFTERWORD

Gentle Reader,

The last line goes to Robert Louis Stevenson, as well it should.

My hijacking of his masterpiece began innocently as a private writing exercise. Like many readers I had affectionate memories of *Treasure Island* that dated back to summer reading, English class, several movie versions, and the Classic Comic. Rereading it recently, with a dozen thrillers, mysteries, and sea stories to my credit—and a thirteenth novel foundering in the typewriter, which was why I was ransacking the classics—I was struck envious by Stevenson's extraordinary story speed. Here was a bold narrator, ever on the move, yet always honoring his descriptive responsibilities.

I wondered whether I could learn some narrative tricks by updating his first chapter. If I could sail briefly in company with the master, maybe I could figure out how he hurtled his lively characters through such rich settings.

Stevenson had started his story on an English coast, a hundred or so years before the time he was writing, and set it within the frame of a man recounting his boyhood. I moved it a similar distance ahead of Stevenson's life, to my boyhood on the Great South Bay of the 1950s.

To compare my exercise to refitting a sailing vessel with a modern powerplant is not accurate, as Mr. Stevenson has no need of improved propulsion. In fact, updating a nineteenth-century writer's version of eighteenth-century English proved more like translating from a foreign language. Particularly as sea lore represented the high technology of the day. Having cleared the decks of archaic English with the help of *Webster's Second*, *Chamber's Dictionary*, and *The Concise Scots Dictionary*, I learned a thing or two about writing. But mainly I had fun. More fun than I was having with the sinking novel. So I translated Chapter Two. By the end of the third chapter my literary agent, Henry Morrison, was questioning my career goals, if not my sanity.

After eight chapters, he was hooked, too. He and my sister Alison Skelton gave me some good advice to break loose from Stevenson's language. My friend Jim Frye helped solve the "Yo-ho-ho, and a bottle of rum!" problem with his wonderful suggestion of the old U.S. Philippine Army's, "Oh the monkeys have no tails in Zamboanga." That song freed me from Stevenson's time, though not, of course, his genius. (Readers who notice how I stuck to structure, sentence by sentence, paragraph by paragraph, should know that when my modern instincts provoked me to rearrange the order of events, I usually discovered Mr. Stevenson's instincts the more reliable.)

When I was done, my agent ventured into the marketplace with instructions to find me a brave publisher. He did. The result is in your hands, a hundred years after a great writer died young on Samoa—his story for "modern" men and women who once were boys and girls.

—JUSTIN SCOTT